GW00728995

ELSEWHERE

ELSEWHERE

The Adventures of Belemus
by
Sebastian Barry

Drawings by
Raymond Mullan

BROGEEN BOOKS
THE DOLMEN PRESS

Set in Plantin type and assembled by Design and Art Facilities Limited,
Dublin and printed for the publishers,
By O'Brien Promotions Limited

BROGEEN BOOKS
The Dolmen Press Limited
Mountrath Portlaoise Ireland

Designed by Liam Miller

First published 1985
ISBN 085105 9031

The Dolmen Press receives financial assistance from
The Arts Council, An Comhairle Ealaion, Ireland.

First paperback edition published in 1997 by
Colin Smythe Limited, P.O.Box 6,
Gerrards Cross, Buckinghamshire SL9 8XA

ISBN 0-85105-904-X

Text © 1985 Sebastian Barry
Illustrations © 1985 The Dolmen Press Ltd.

Copyright under the Berne Convention, all rights reserved. Apart from fair
dealing for study or review, no part of this publication may be reproduced,
stored in a retrieval system, or transmitted in any form or by any means,
electronic, mechanical, photocopying, recording, or otherwise, without the
prior permission of the Dolmen Press.

CONTENTS

Chapter

I	The Last King	*page* 9
II	The Poor Skull	18
III	The White North	23
IV	The Storm	31
V	Mister Creek's Secret	48
VI	The Little Gods	62
VII	The Cave	72
VIII	The Roundabout Way	77
IX	The Case of the Stately Borzoi	86
X	The Setting Sun	104
XI	Under the Cloth	114

ILLUSTRATIONS

"He drew back from the edge of the stone,
gesturing for his son to follow him"   *page* 15

"The skull cried briefly, white dried tears like
blobs of dust"   19

"I was silently thanking my mother when the
bear stepped out in front of me"   29

"Not so good, Belemus, we're in a wide lageen here
in this part, and there's no island near till evening"   37

"The mast keeled…"   43

"'That Mr Creek be an old humbug, he be,'
she muttered, 'should be butchered orf, by Gord'"   50

"I fell forward and everything passed out of
my reckoning"   59

"They came bowling down the hill"   67

"One of the oaks went on fire"   73

"Pardon me?"   91

"I got him. I got Ned Bailey"   113

"The captain's head grew big again, and the eyes
of the parasite closed"   126

for
Hazel McGilligan

'I call in the boy,
Have him sit on his knees here
        To seal this,
And send it a thousand miles, thinking.'

from EXILE'S LETTER,
by Ezra Pound

I THE LAST KING

I LOOKED out my window, and the sun was shining. My family was joking and laughing at breakfast because they liked the good weather too.

At twenty past eight I hurried down our steps, and ran round the corner, and crossed the wide road. It seemed a pity to be going to school on such a rare day. I waited at the bus-stop. The woman with the white pony-tail, who lives across from the shop, put her nose out her door. I heard the roar of an engine in the distance. I could see the tall bus pull around the bend at the top of the hill before it did. I suppose I was used to it.

The woman came out on her front steps. The bus bowled down the hill. She dashed over the road, waving all the time to the blank house behind her. I put out my hand. The brakes screamed like a cat. The woman and I poised. She leaped and I leaped. I reached the platform and was surrounded by hills.

There were birds singing in the small trees and a sound in the clay of grasshoppers and what books call cicadas. The hills were rocky and brown, and the lower parts of them were terraced and had vines growing in the rectangular fields. I saw gentle plumes of smoke, coming up straight from hidden farms.

The sun was high above me, giving off a steady sleepy heat. I heard a dog barking angrily. I left my school-bag by a rock and went in the direction of the noise.

I came on a narrow path. It had black droppings on it every few feet. There were rabbits at the edge from time to time and they scuttled off into the undergrowth.

The path wound this way and that. There were bushes with flowers like yellow and red stars, and tall blooms with a sprinkle of white swords spreading from the top.

I came to a paved terrace – a rough affair with the rim of each flagstone painted white. In front of me was a white dwelling with five pillars. The dog was somewhere behind it. I couldn't see him, but he was barking in a mad sort of way.

He stopped, and a boy of my age walked out onto the terrace from the house, taking the long flight of steps slowly, and looking into my eyes with a little smile. The smile was odd and I couldn't decide whether it was a friendly one or what.

Behind the boy a man stepped out and sat down in a stone chair. He was dressed in a white tunic with a gold edge to the hem and the collar. There was something strong about him.

'So you decided to come,' said the boy, still looking into my face. I was almost hypnotised by it, and by his voice, which was like the water of a pool.

'Well, yes,' I said, 'sort of. I suppose so.'

'This is what we like,' said the boy, 'faithfulness, loyalty. It is the only way.'

'I agree,' I said.

'It is not for you to agree,' the boy corrected me. 'Only to obey.'

That made me feel uncomfortable, but I didn't laugh at him. He said his words so naturally that I began to feel as solemn as he looked.

The dog barked again. The man on the chair struck his hand on the arm of the seat, and the bark stopped.

'The others will be here soon,' said the boy. 'Perhaps tonight. Tomorrow we do the thing for which you were summoned. Then you return to your farm. This place is for kings and the sons of kings. I trust you have made your ablutions?'

I think that's what he said, but the last word puzzled me. I suppose I must have nodded – I hate admitting I don't know what a word means – because he seemed satisfied.

'Good,' he said. 'You must call me Little Master.'

'Okay,' I said. 'You can call me Belemus.'

'That is your name?'

I should explain that my father is a professor. He

10

teaches Latin at the university. So he gave us these strange names. My sister is called Cordelia, though that isn't really to do with Latin, but some play by Shakespeare. But our family name is Duck, which is mixing the sublime with the ridiculous, if you know the phrase.

'Yes,' I admitted. 'It is. I'm Belemus Duck.'

'It is the sort of name one expects for a farmer's son,' said the Little Master.

He brought me up to the house and gave me a bowl of water and some bread. I thought since I had just finished breakfast I wouldn't want it, but I did. It tasted good. The boy stood watching me, staring at my eyes as if he were worried they were going to disappear if he didn't.

'This is your lord,' he said, gesturing with his forehead at the man in the chair. 'Your Big Master. You must kiss his toes.'

Well, the Big Master was there on his throne, and his big feet were at the ends of his long legs. They looked clean enough, those large brown toes. I gave the boy a quick glance to see if he were joking. He didn't seem to be. The Big Master was expecting something, because I saw one of his toes twitch.

'It is all right,' the Big Master said, in a voice like a waterfall. 'It is only the custom. To blow my feet a kiss will be enough. I see, though I do not look at you, that you are a rarer boy than most. I wonder to myself which farm and what part of my kingdom you come from.'

That sounded complimentary and it would have been silly not even to blow a kiss. So I did.

'Do you, perhaps,' said the Big Master – now that he was speaking the Little Master was looking at him not at me – 'come from the Southern Province? The Rich Coast, perhaps?'

'No, I don't think so,' I said. 'I came straight from the bus-stop.'

'The buzztop,' said the Big Master. 'A town I haven't heard of. The Buzztop. This is a puzzle. I know all my properties. But not this one.'

'Well it's to the east,' I said, thinking of Dublin being on the east coast of Ireland, 'you know what the East's like. A bit of a jumble.'

'At any rate you answered the albatross,' said the Big Master. 'It is enough.'

As he said that, a bird like a sea-gull, on a larger scale, came slanting down from the sky and turned and turned in circles over the house. The boy jumped out onto the terrace in excitement. It was the first time he looked like a real boy, with his face lit with a laugh and his arms waving.

'He returns!' he shouted. 'Gadoc returns!'

'The tribe is gathering,' said the Big Master. 'We shall soon be strong for the fight.'

The albatross stayed up in the air, with a drawn-out cry. The Little Master went silent. The Big Master rose from his chair, and gazed up into the blue air at the bird.

'What is it?' the Little Master asked him.

'They betray us. No one comes,' the man said.

'Honour has fled the country,' said the boy.

'They are worthless,' said the Big Master. 'They grow rich and desert me. The old ways are dying.'

'Some day they will need your strength again,' said the boy, looking up at his father.

'So,' said the man. 'We must do the work without them.'

'I suppose,' said the boy, 'we must be thankful one at least came to aid his king.'

He looked at me. I should have bowed to him just to cheer him up, but I didn't.

'Come within,' the king said to me, 'we shall talk of the fight.'

The three of us entered the wide doors of the house and went over to a long table in the centre of the room. The four walls were rough and painted white, and the table was made of a black wood like oak. There were exactly fifty-two chairs, twenty-five on each side, and one at each

12

end of the table more elaborate than the others. I counted them as the Little Master laid water and bread and fruit in lonely groups at three of the places. We each had our separate food, because the table was so big. I saw that there were more goblets, and urns of water, and plates of bread and fruit. I was sorry for them that their followers hadn't bothered to answer the albatross.

The king and his son took their places at the opposite ends of the table and I sat down at about the centre where the boy had put the food. I liked them more now because they weren't the sort of kings that like everything done for them. Since I was the only one to have turned up they were treating me better, and the boy was staring into my eyes only when he forgot himself.

'The Moks,' said the Big Master, 'will be passing through our domain in the morning. They are travelling to their new fortress in the Gentle Hills. The Albatross circled them two days ago, but they did not call him to fasten the king's tribute to his leg. Yet still they move through my lands, and care nothing for honour. They eat the bread of my farmers. They talk with them like equals. The old days are going. The Albatross is weighed down by sadness. Soon he will no longer fly above our house. He will return to the North.'

'Father,' said the boy, 'we will take their power from them, and leave them with their naked souls. We shall wrest their Book from their saddle-bag.'

'It will be difficult with three,' said the Big Master. 'But it must be done. Honour is all, as is innocence. We must return our country to the old ways, or die.'

'We will not die, father,' the Little Master said.

I slept that night outside between the pillars, on a hammock. I was thinking as I lay there of the funny way the Little and the Big Master talked with each other. It seemed ancient. They never said things like 'Pass the salt,' or 'Isn't it a nice night,' they only spoke when it was something of importance to them. They were so stately

13

and different to me, with my gray school trousers, and gray jumper with the red line at the neck.

The king was sleeping in the house, but I could see his son out on the terrace, curled up on the bare stone. He was crying now and then quickly, like a night bird. That was a sound I knew, it's the sound you make when you're dreaming a nightmare and you can't wake up. I lay under the big sky of stars, with a white moon, listening to the boy and wondering where I was.

The morning seemed to come fast. The night was long, but no more than ten minutes. I didn't sleep. I rested there while the time went on and on for hours that were only minutes.

The first sheet of the sun crept in over the hill, covering up the shadows, and the Little Master stirred in his sleep. The warm sun touched him and lit his head. He started from his dreams like an animal, and looked around him with fierceness. I was relieved when he calmed down, because I was afraid he'd see and not recognise me, and go for my throat.

He shook off the look as he walked towards me. I slipped from the hammock. He was quiet, but nodded at me like a friend. He touched my shoulder and passed into the house. He returned with food for us both. We sat without talking on the white steps, watching the sun roll into the sky. I was warm and frightened.

After breakfast the king came out from the house with a silver dish. He brought it to the middle of the terrace where there was a square stone set in among the rest.

He put down the bowl – which shook with the light of the sun – and drew a knife from his tunic. It was gold, with a handle of brown metal. The king slid the blade against the skin of his thumb, with his eyes closed, and I waited in a horror for the blood to drop into the dish. But either the knife had not cut him, or there was something else involved, because no blood came. The king opened his eyes to look at his thumb, and the only thing that fell

"He drew back from the edge of the stone, gesturing for his son to follow him"

into the bowl was his tears.

The Little Master fetched a collection of arms. There were short swords with thin blades, and tall spears with carvings of birds and men in tunics. All the time, from the moment they had woken up, the two, father and son, hadn't spoken, and I didn't like to break that silence. I took the spear and the sword that the Little Master gave me, and watched while they chose their weapons from the bundle. The ones that weren't chosen they dropped on the terrace.

I followed them across their domain. We came to a place where a road entered a narrow valley and wandered among hanging rocks and scraggy trees. There was no sunlight in the gorge because the sides were too steep to get the morning light. There was a cool watery air about it. The king and his son walked with straight backs, and their heads held up.

We went off the road further in and climbed through the bushes and the rocks to a flat stone that overlooked a stretch of the road below. Some trees and rocks had been cleared so you could view the road and yet be unseen yourself. We sat on the white stone.

After a while the sun began to find its way into the gorge and it grew hot. I could see the king had beads of sweat on his forehead. Once the boy flicked a little black spider from his arm and looked up in fright at his father.

I heard a noise from the edge of the valley below us, and I jumped. They heard the sound as well, a tinkle of harness, and lay flat on their stomachs. In a few minutes we saw the first horse and rider. The group of Moks was as silent as we were – perhaps they were on their guard. After a bit I could see them clearly, when they came out from the shade of the trees.

The men on their small ponies were dressed in brown tunics, and some of them had their hoods up on their heads, in the heat. Around their waists they wore belts of rope, and at their sides hung crosses. They rode slowly, separate from the things around them, robed and hooded away into a private world. They neither looked up the sides of the valley to spot danger, nor behind them. They had no weapons that I could see. It was clear that the king was surprised. He wanted to rush down and restore the old ways but I think he got a new smell from the Moks that he hadn't got before. I began to think of this name he had given them, and guessed that he had heard it from some clumsy-speaking farmer, because the men below us on the track were not a wild set of tribesmen, but monks.

It seemed as if we were poised there for ever and ever, the ponies with the monks always coming on along the path, the king and the Little Master and I for ever watching them approach.

The monk in front had a book slung on his saddle-bag, a thick black book like a church bible. I saw the king look at it carefully, even respectfully, as it bounced a bit under the pony's walk. He looked again at the peaceful unheeding monks and suddenly at me, and at my strange clothes from the 'East', from a town in his kingdom he hadn't even heard of. I wonder what he thought. He drew back from the edge of the stone, gesturing for his son to follow him.

I almost went with them, but I hesitated. They slipped away with their swords and spears into the thick net of thorns, and I heard them moving higher and higher into the gorge. With a wave of sadness I turned to go after them, but when I moved I was back beside my schoolbag, and when I moved again in bewilderment, I was sitting at my desk in school.

The clock on the wall said four o'clock. Everyone around me was fidgeting and rustling, and the master was too, the way he does when the bell's about to go to finish school.

17

II   THE POOR SKULL

I T WAS raining next morning so I got off at Hewett's garage. I can walk from there along the Grand Canal – it's the quickest way to school when it's wet. Sometimes I see swans as I pass the black lock.

The raincoats of the passers-by and the goers-in-my-direction were turning a dark gray. I trudged along with my school-bag. The big old houses of Leeson Street looked like sick friends – they should have been in bed with lemon drinks and hot-water bottles.

I was walking along the pavement past one of the street-lamps, noticing the dirt on it, when I found myself elsewhere.

There were two things around me – tar and sky. I put down my school-bag. The tar stretched away on each side. It was hard and black.

I began to walk. I walked so far my bag was a leather dot behind me. There wasn't a tree or a house. I saw in the distance a little stick. As I got closer I could see the stick had a square top on it – it was a notice-board. It looked like the only notice-board that had ever existed. It said:

DO NOT WALK ON THE TAR
By Order

I went round to the other side of the sign. That said:

KEEP TO THE GRASS
By Order

I knelt and gazed at the tar. Could there be grass growing on it that I couldn't see? But that would still be breaking the rule.

'This is silly,' I said aloud.

'You're right,' said a voice.

"The skull cried briefly, white dried tears like blobs of dust"

A bulldozer appeared and rushed about from horizon to horizon. In half a minute it had paths dozed all over, and even before it had disappeared again, there was fine grass pushing its way up.

'It's still silly,' I said. 'Everything's back to front. The tar should be where the grass is.'

'Oh no,' said the voice. 'We try to have beautiful parks here.'

It was while I was having this conversation with the voice that I started to wonder whom it belonged to. A skull dropped from the sky and I was both surprised and not surprised. He landed on the notice-board and clacked his teeth.

'Phew,' he said, 'a safe landing. Usually I lose a few old molars. You must appreciate how much I like them, and how ready they are to fall out.'

'Does this park belong to you?' I said.

'In a way,' he said. 'But nothing belongs to anyone. We share. We're so busy sharing, we don't own anything.'

'This sign,' I said, 'it didn't make sense when I arrived.'

'It's a new sign. It's a new park. They're all the same these notice-boards. They come from a factory. The factory signs say the same thing. You have to make the park to suit the sign these days.'

The skull cried briefly, white dry tears like blobs of dust.

'It is unfortunate,' I said.

The skull and I looked at the expanse of tar, with the splendid grass paths crossing and recrossing it.

'Maybe,' he said wistfully, 'we'll be able to change it back some day.'

The thought of this was so strong for him that he burst into fresh sprinkles of sandy weeping, and he laughed:

'Still,' he said, 'it's lovely to see a new... well, a new face. We can't all be handsome.'

That was polite of the skull.

'Do come,' he said, 'and have a glass of dust. It will refresh you. It was raining this morning. It was

20

exhausting. I'm all moistured up.'

'I'd be pleased to,' I said, thinking I'd sit and watch the skull drinking, and pour my dust surreptitiously into a flowerpot like they do in the cinema – if there was a flowerpot.

'Come on then,' he said, and vanished overhead.

I felt silly.

The skull slipped back a few seconds later and said:

'Are you awaiting someone then?'

'No, no,' I said. 'I just don't know how to... to disappear.'

'Good heavens,' he said. 'Nothing to it. Just blow on your tongue.'

'Oh,' I said.

I curled my tongue and got air blown at it as best I could. I rose to the level of the skull. I looked down at my legs and they weren't there. My arms were gone too. I and the skull, wherever he was – I could hear his teeth clacking – went up and up through the gray sky. There was a smell of burnt rubber or burnt something-or-other, a kind of passing-a-factory smell.

We came up among warm hills. There were sunny woods, and rivers with trout jumping in them, and a light everywhere, a late evening light. It made me want to sit down and scratch the ground. I said:

'Gosh.'

'I know,' said the skull. 'It's no one's fault. It's this business of sharing. We tried, some of us, to stop it, but it gets worse every year. A new wood here, a fresh river there, and every week, every week, they go out and pull up more roads and plant all sorts of rare trees and even unmentionable things like beehives.'

I realised how it was with the skull, so I hid my pleasure.

We strolled over the lush grass – or rather I strolled and the skull spun.

'Who takes the roads and tar away?' I said.

'Oh we do,' he said. 'I suppose it's more convenient and

clean. But it isn't the same. It isn't beautiful. And my park's ruined too.'

'I'm sorry,' I said. I was, and I tried to show him I meant it.

'It's not your fault,' he said. 'When they gave me the park to design I wanted to leave it as it was. Few skulls have time to visit parks. But I expect some idle fellow would have rolled up eventually. A matter of time. For our beautiful tar it's always a matter of time. Progress, you know.'

'I know,' I said.

'Well,' said the skull, 'here's my house. I'm sorry it's so much a mansion. They just aren't building high-rise flats any more.'

His house was hidden in trees, old trees with lichened trunks. A marble terrace led up to his door. It was strange to see the poor skull labouring up the steps, and sighing all the time, and trying to nudge open the tall wooden entrance.

'Oh these places are so killing,' he said. I pushed the door for him and we went in.

I wasn't to get dust to drink after all. I stepped in and was back beside my school-bag. I lifted it up. I headed again towards the notice-board but didn't get two yards before I was sitting in class, with O'Donnell half-asleep beside me, and the hands of the clock tipping round to four.

III THE WHITE NORTH

O NE MONDAY the skies were thick and gray. I
looked out my window and the terrace was covered
in a blue-white sleep of snow. The cars had new roofs
made of it, and the wall dividing the low road from the
upper was half a foot higher. I watched the postman
wheel his bicycle past our door, making a wavy line with
his wheels. The milkman pulled round the corner and his
horse was steamy and slow, with flowers of white smoke
blowing from the nostrils. He's a pleasant horse. He
walks from house to house without the milkman having
to tell him. He never goes too far or too slowly. The milkman swings the bottles off, and the horse draws onwards.
I hear the man talk and sing, and there's only the horse to
listen.

We ate breakfast in the kitchen because it was warmer
there. My father was doing the breakfast so we all kept
quiet and out of his way. He's a perfectionist when it
comes to rashers and eggs, and if you block his path when
he's twirling round the oven you get a roar that rattles the
bits that tie your ears on.

I plucked up my school-bag from the hall and went out
on the top of the steps. The air was thinner than a little
biscuit – it made me feel as awake as an otter.

I kept my head down to watch the steps, which were
under snow. On the last step I put my foot down too
quickly and pitched forward onto the pavement.

I got up. I noticed a slight wind that wasn't there
before. It had begun to snow. The cars on the terrace
were gone, and the wall. I was going to push on around
the corner to the bus-stop, but that was gone too, along
with the houses and the families eating breakfast. There
was the little wind and the snow coming down in a steady
fall. I clutched my school-bag tighter, and didn't feel like
putting it down.

As I stood there in the stillness, the snow thinned and
thinned and stopped. A blue light crept from the ground,

and spread across the sky. It was like daylight, but I don't think it was, because there was a large white moon taking up a lot of the sky.

Beside me was a hump made from ice, an igloo. In the entrance a brown face was looking out at me, and the tip of a spear beside it. I gave the old man a nod to show I was friendly, and shuddered with cold.

The old man made up his mind and stepped out. He pointed back into the igloo, and I went over and ducked inside. He followed me, letting a flap of leather fall over the entrance.

It was as warm as skin in the tiny house. He had bowls of liquid, with tapers of string, burning strongly, which gave off a light that made the icy wall glisten. There were skins and spears about the wall and floor, and in the darkest part was a tent of leather where an ancient woman was sitting.

The man clapped his hands, and took my bag from me. He propped it against the wall, gave it a pat, and looked over at me. I liked him. He had a frightening face, with slitted eyes that seemed always to be squeezed against a wind, and a thousand wrinkles in his skin. His hands were brown and hard-looking. When he touched my face to see what the white skin felt like, it was I who was as cold as snow. His wrinkled hand was as warm as the fender of a fire.

He gave me a length of dried meat, and there was plenty of water from dried snow. The wife crouched in her tent of skin and summed me up. After a while the old man got up and brushed out of the igloo. For the next hour or so I and the woman squatted without speaking.

The man rushed in and beckoned me to follow him. I said good-bye to the woman and she smiled.

Outside the weather was holding, and the moon and sky was spread over us. There was a sledge by the door with four dogs harnessed up to it. They were milling around, getting themselves knotted in the leashes, and barking with a sound like trees falling. The old man made

24

them straighten out and gave them an order to be still. I wondered where he had got them and I was grateful.

He laced a pair of snow-shoes under my soles, and showed me how to stand at the back of the sledge to steer it. He went into the igloo and came out with my school-bag and some lengths of meat and tossed them into the carrier of the sledge. The only thing I knew about driving it apart from what the man showed me was that Eskimos always say 'Mush! Mush!' to their dogs in the cinema. I hoped that that would be right for these tangly huskies.

The man pressed his cheek against mine, and in a stony language seemed to wish me luck in my journey. There was a look in his eyes that told me I was far from anywhere. I tried to ask him which direction to take, and he pointed his hand towards the moon. I supposed I was to keep straight for it. He patted my arm, and with an effort of memory said:

'Dogs know.'

He gave a shout to the huskies, and the sledge pulled away with me perched on it, and I was trying hard to keep it from spinning over. I looked back once, and the man was standing without waving beside the house.

The dogs were good now, and ran straight. I shouted out 'Mush! Mush!' now and then in case they wanted to hear it. They neither stopped nor quickened when I shouted, they just forged on. They ran swiftly considering there were only four of them, their paws sending up a skither of soft snow. The sledge flashing over the ground made a noise like knives being sharpened.

We seemed to be passing over a broad plain. It was flat and big, and the dogs had no trouble. After a hard hour of running, I got them to stop, because I remembered how our dog's paws get in snow. I checked the huskies' paws and there were clogs of ice between the pads. I cleaned all sixteen feet, and gave each dog a pat and a tear of meat, and we went on.

We came to the end of the great plain, and started to

bump and swerve through a field of humpy snow. The humps grew larger and larger, and the dogs had to struggle and pull to get the sledge through. I got off the running-board and pushed with them, bounding into the air when the sledge twisted.

Walls of snow surrounded us on either side, and I felt like I was in the delved-out hills of a railway track. I was hot, with my anorak zipped and laced. The snow-shoes were hard to walk in, and sometimes I fell forward and got my face smothered. It was fun the first time, as if the land was playing with me. It soon began to tire me out. I knew there was to be no stopping. I didn't know how to build an igloo, and I had no wood for a fire in the treeless land.

We were pushing and heaving through a difficult patch when I saw slabs of ice floating in a dark sea. Out in the bay icebergs were drifting. The dogs didn't care, and took a course at the edge of the frozen floors. They sped over one that was locked against the shore, and I felt the surface dipping as our weight passed over it.

The dogs hurried on, barking to keep their spirits up. I was tired. I was sweating inside, but chilly on my face and hands. I could hardly feel my hands at all. In front of us I could see the white shore and the curves and inlets of the sea.

I thought I saw a ship far out in the bay. It was a black shape like a beetle, way off on the horizon. I imagined I could hear the catly purr of its engines. I stood on the snow and roared and waved, and the ship shrunk and shrunk to nothing and disappeared. The dogs didn't understand my shouting. I made to step on the sledge and they pulled it on away from me and wouldn't let me up. I talked to them, but they were more than half decided against me. I made a grab for the sledge and missed. They took off. They swung in a curve and headed back the way we had come. The sledge hit a bump and spun over. The dogs whined in surprise. My school-bag and the meat spilled out, and the sledge balanced sideways at the edge of the sea. The huskies strained to keep it from slipping in.

I stumbled over. The dogs didn't care about me anymore, all they wanted was to escape the sea. I worked as quickly as my fingers would let me, freeing the toiling animals from their harness. I had to be careful when I had the first two free, because that meant there were only two left to keep up the sledge. With one hand I gripped the contraption – which was slipping an inch or two all the time – and with the other I untied the third dog. It was I and the last dog then, and I thought my arm would be wrenched off. The sledge was small but it seemed to weigh as much as an aeroplane. I thought the last dog was done for when the sledge began to slide quickly. I could hear the sea-water lapping at it. I held onto it by the harness, my other numb hand tearing at the final knots. The dog was frantic, yelping like a child, its feet down in the snow from its efforts. I got the knots untied, and the dog bounced forward like a bird. The sledge paused a moment. It tipped back and sank.

I turned to the huskies. They were happily eating the last of the dried meat. I think they would have eaten my leather school-bag too if I hadn't snatched it up. The gesture of snatching reminded them that they didn't trust me, and they set off again, paws flying, for home.

I decided as I looked about me that I had to keep moving. A minute standing still in that climate had begun to chill my bones. I supposed I must follow the coastline, keeping the moon in front of me as often as I could.

With my school-bag slung on my shoulder I blundered on. I remembered the packet of sandwiches that I had for lunch, and as I walked I unclasped my bag and had a look. My mother had packed an orange for me too, and a bottle of lemonade. I unwrapped the silver paper and had one of the beef sandwiches, and washed it down with a swig of lemonade. I was silently thanking my mother when the bear stepped out in front of me.

He was a tall white bear, with a long pair of arms which he had spread out to block my way. I suppose he had just been strolling along, and was as surprised as I was to come across another animal. I tried not to move, but in my fright my school-bag fell from my shoulder. The bear lurched forward at me and vanished through the ground in a flurry of flakes.

I looked carefully into the hold he had made in the whiteness. He was roaring in a narrow ravine. It seemed in the dim light to go down for ever, but in the depths, about twenty feet below, I could hear water splashing about.

The bear was stranded on a ledge half-way down. He was pawing and struggling to get out. When he stretched full-height his paws were only a foot from the edge of the surface. He wasn't able to climb out.

I got over the relief that his attack on me had failed, and was struck by the fact that if he hadn't blocked my path it would be me trapped on the ledge, or frozen to death in the water at the bottom. The bear calmed for a while, and swayed and turned on the ledge to cheer himself up. Maybe he had meant to save me falling in, and the bag dropping had frightened him. Most of my instincts told me to leave him to his fate and continue on myself, but I started to dig. I sat on the snow, and worked away at the rim of the ravine with my feet so that slowly a slope was being made for the bear to climb out on. The snow dropped on top of him, and he didn't like that and thought I was trying to bury him. But the skites of snow fell on down past him into the water.

When he found he could get his paws onto the slope I was making, he started to drag more snow away with swipes of his arms. He was ruining my plan, so I had to begin pushing snow away from a point further back. Between him and me we made two steps in the snow and in another few minutes he was able to pull himself from

"I was silently thanking my mother when the bear stepped out in front of me"

the ledge to the first step and, with a burst of white from his shoulders and head, out into the air again.

This time I didn't move. He stood quietly, and looked back into the ravine and at me.

He went down on his four feet, and turned his back to me. He made odd grunts, backing up till his fur touched my trousers and anorak. Hoping I wasn't misinterpreting him I picked up my school-bag and scrambled onto his back. It was like climbing on a bony table – he was thin under his thick fur. I held on by tufts and with another grunt he ambled forward.

We travelled the rest of the day and didn't stop. The moon never left the sky, and there was always the half-darkness over the snow. He brought me across floating platforms, and up into a region of glaciers. We passed through a valley, and I could see, away at the top of the mountains, clumps of cloud stuck on the peaks like ships. We came to a ravine and the bear broke into a powerful run. I hung on like a koala to its mother, and when the bear leaped my heart leaped forward with him.

At the last pass in the mountains he halted. Below us in the snowy plain was a group of buildings. A tall aerial was rising out of the middle of them, and the houses were not made of ice but metal, which flashed at us dully in the moonlight. The bear could go no further. I climbed from his back with my bag and we stood on the snow. He turned his head in a long swing and ran in rocking strides back to the mountains.

Plodding in my snow-shoes I started to walk down into the plain. As I got closer I noticed there was a flag flying from the top of the biggest building, an American one. I heard stray wisps of music from a radio playing in the camp, some instrument like a trumpet. I felt a bit silly in my anorak and with my school-bag on my shoulder, walking in out of the wilds. I wondered what the Americans would say, and how I would get home. I supposed they would call for a helicopter, or whatever

30

they had in those parts.

I passed by a pile of black plastic bags, all neatly tied up, and there was a sign nearly buried in the snow which said:

GARBAGE

I heard the music clearer, and from the open window of the first metal dome I caught laughter and a voice saying:

'Damn right!'

I put out my hand to turn the handle. It wasn't surprised scientists that I saw inside, but a flood of boys. It was the corridor of my school, and we were pouring from the class-rooms on our way home.

IV THE STORM

IF I'M a bit fed-up with the bus I walk – in the other direction – down the terrace, and cross the road to the sea front. There's a green bridge that goes over the railway track, and I follow a concrete path on the other side till I get to the Martello Tower. I go round that and down along a little street of villas that face the sea and Dublin Bay, and hitch open a wooden gate to the station platform. I get a yellow ticket there for sixpence that takes me into town.

That morning I especially wanted to take the train because I had noticed from my bedroom that there was a great crowd of white horses in the bay and that meant spray. Spray down on our sea front means big waves coming hard to the sea-wall and smashing up into columns and boulders of water.

As I crossed the green bridge a fat wind rattled at my shirt – it was warm that day despite the storm – and I could taste the salt moisture in the air. Our inlet was like a ploughed field of green and white ridges that were moving one after the other to the battered wall. I ran along the concrete path.

I came out on the sea-wall and looked for the places where the waves would hit most fiercely. I wondered were there any ships out in this weather, because it was unusually bad – or good in my view – even for spring. I managed to get the length of the wall without being drenched, except that at the last a funny little wave slopped up and wet my knees. I laughed at my almost complete victory and headed on along the road that has the villas to the station. I got in the gate and bent down to tie my lace and found no shoes on my feet, my trousers gray-white and baggy, and a scrubbing brush in my fist. I looked up and saw about me the tar-smelling deck of a sailing-ship.

It was warm, and I no longer had a shirt on. There was a sun like the devil up in the sky, and a red glow at the line of the horizon. There was a man standing at the wooden rail near me, watching the sea. He wasn't leaning idly, but straining slightly forward trying to ascertain something. He was dressed like me, but with a wide leather belt around his waist, and a yellowed shirt. I stood up from my scrubbing, and poured my bucket of water into the sea.

'It be strange, Duck me lad. Strange,' said the man, looking out over the flat hot sea. There was nothing around us except water and the occasional bird among the rigging. A breeze was filling the canvas sails, and the ship was pulling along with a steady purling from the prow.

Top Harry – I knew this man was called Top Harry, I can't say how – shook his head, and pointed a gnarled finger. I followed the direction of his hand till I noticed a slight commotion on the water. It was like a circle of fine lace, twenty feet in circumference, moving and slipping over the water in silence. Some quirk of the wind was holding it up like a curtain, and it was spinning round and

round. It kept a course on past the ship, and swirled off
into the distance. Top Harry looked down at me, and his
red rummy face nodded in agreement with himself:

'Funny weather a-comin', boy. We'll see a Guy Fawkes
today, I don't doubt.' We gazed over the blue sea,
wondering how long the bad weather would take in
coming.

'Better tell your cap'ain to come up, Duck lad. The
sails'll need figurin'.'

I spun away from the rail and hung my bucket and
brush on their brass hook by the galley. I could hear the
cook inside making his eternal stew, and saw his dirty
steam belch out of the tin chimney on top. I ducked down
the middle hatch and clattered to the bottom of the stairs.
There was a narrow passage where the rich paying-
passengers had their cabins, but I turned back the other
side of the stairs to go forward to the Captain's quarters.
He had his own hatch up forward on the deck, but no one
was allowed to use it. He hated meeting anyone in the
morning below decks – or anytime.

I passed through the main hold. We were carrying a
cargo of white horses, mares and one stallion. There was
a sailor to look after them, a man who had been a
muleteer in the Mexican Army. He was a bashed man
with one eye, or as he said, half an eye, which he thought
meant the same thing. He slept most of the time, on a pile
of horse-rugs in a dark corner of the hold, so he could
wake up in time if the Captain was passing through.

The horses were handsome fellows, with lovely glisten-
ing coats. I suppose the Muleteer must have brushed
them up pretty well, but I never caught him doing it. The
stallion in particular, with his thick neck and his fierce
narrow head, was a horse to own if you wanted to travel
fast and in style. He and the mares were all in separate
stalls that the carpenter had built before we set out from
the last Asian port, and were tethered and tied with ropes,
though they had a bit of freedom to step backward and

33

forward. We were running a five-day journey to the next big port, through an area of that sea called the White Archipelago, that is to say a place where the islands had fine white beaches.

I saw the Muleteer dimly in his corner asleep, and pushed on through into the Captain's corridor. His stateroom was at the end, after the six doors that were our store-rooms. I knocked timidly on his oaken door. Carved above the cross-beam was:

STATEROOM
1789

I heard a half-growl from the interior, and I turned the heavy handle. I put my nose around the door. I could see nothing but a big screwed-down table, a row of dazzling windows that followed the vee-shape of the ship's prow, and shelves and shelves of leather-bound books. There was a large globe of the world, and a variety of ships' instruments and maps on the top of the desk. Then I saw the Captain in his patched armchair to the right of the door. He had his shining shoes off – how often I had rubbed them into glowing form – and his linen socks, and was rubbing at his hard yellow feet with a pumice-stone. The Captain took great care of his appearance, in readiness, as he told me, for the Port Ladies.

He had not much hair to speak of though, the Captain, apart from shocking eyebrows like bushes and a big Swedish-looking moustache. He called the moustache his Dundrearies, and he was proud of them, whatever he meant by it. I suppose all in all he was a good Captain, because he had the respect of his men, and kept his oddities to his cabin. Whenever he emerged from his hatch above he was a hard and forbidding man, and you jumped to it when he barked an order. But I liked him best when he was in his quarters, and indeed I was the only one who could carry any information down to him with any safety. A cabin-boy didn't count much in his reckoning of things.

He glanced over at me and said:

'Belemus, is it? Well, Belemus, since we can't afford to send you to school, would you be so kind as to fetch me that basin of hot water.'

He always said things like that, 'Belemus, since you won't be thirteen till next year, would you peel me that apple', and so on. He had a basin of water in the sun on one of the window-sills, and the hot light had warmed it up nicely. I brought it over to him and he gave me a small smile. It was a pity about the Captain's face, in regard to the Port Ladies, because his nose was the most awful long hook I've ever seen, like a prince from Florence, the cook said. And maybe the Captain had been a prince there once.

'You know, Belemus,' said the Captain, 'I've sat here often working on my feet, and the more I work the yellower they get, and the yellower they get the older I feel.'

'Captain, Top Harry says there's weather coming up.'

'Weather? Well now, with horses on board that'll be a plank. Bales of this and that and bad weather is just a sailor's job. But soft-fleshed animals, Belemus, there a sailor must be a father too.'

He washed his large feet clean with the water, and dried them delicately on a fine piece of cloth from the East Indies. I remembered well the time we had carried that cargo, and the merchant making the Captain take a chest of them free, because he liked him.

'Now,' he said, pulling on his socks and shoes with a quickness that always astonished me – because even in the worst emergency he liked to come out on deck fully 'clogged', as Top Harry would say. 'Now my dear boy we must have a strategy for this weather of yours.'

He crossed over to his desk and pulled from a pile a vellum map. He spread it affectionately on the leather desk-top in front of him, and charted with his silver pointers. He drew the day's course in with a pencil, carefully ruling it, and with a sigh or two, as if every mile we sailed on the sea was another mile taken from the course of his life.

'Not so good, Belemus. We're in a wide lagoon here in this part, and there's no island near for till evening. But we'll head in there anyway.'

He left the room abruptly and went up his stairs. I ran back through the hold shouting:

'Weather coming up, Mister Muleteer, look to the horses!'

I shouldn't have done that without the Captain telling me, but I liked to hear the urgency in it.

Out on deck it seemed impossible that there was a storm near. The air was sultry and almost still, just a thick soup of heat lying on your back. I could see the Captain forward talking in low tones with his mate Top Harry, and when I noticed the Captain nodding and not smiling, I knew he agreed with Harry that we were in for something. The wind died away completely, and the red colour on the horizon had spread up further in the sky, till it looked like the banners of an army. The crew were on deck, milling around, the Captain throwing orders to Top Harry, and Top Harry bellowing them at the hands.

'Up, up, boys, get 'em tight true!' he called, and a bunch of men spidered into the rigging to lace in the sails. There were men battening down equipment on the deck, and lashing buckets and such so we wouldn't lose anything in the big sea. They were a good crew that voyage, we had been docked for a solid three months last trip and the Captain had had time to choose a crew with care. I didn't know them well after the scurvy had done for the most of us the last time, and many of my old friends were still sick in port or alas dead. But of course I cabinned with the crew myself, and I was getting to know them more every day, that is to say I knew by now which of

36

"Not so good, Belemus, we're in a wide lagoon here in this part, and there's no island near till evening"

them liked to kick cabin-boys, and which liked to treat them as long lost sons. I suppose to tell the truth I liked Top Harry best, better than the Captain, bcause he treated me straight, and didn't notice too much that I was about thirty years behind him in age.

We stood in that calm for the next two hours. Time at sea is always in hours, or bells or watches, never minutes. The time passes and you pass slowly with it.

Soon the crew had everything shipshape, and the men came down from the sails except for Tom the Raven, the Welshman, who stayed up in the crow's-nest to watch for trouble. Tom the Raven was a bitter man, who never passed me without pulling my hair, or tweaking my tender ears.

It was an odd sight to see the crew standing quiet on the deck, all hands staring forward to spot the storm. It was as if the storm was going to have a face and body. Every time it was like that, the men standing and waiting, and of course the storm would just creep up on us none the less, and not run up in a big sweat like a bull. The Captain kept Top Harry by him, and was pacing the deck peacefully, and the sight of him like that, a bit careless, was keeping the crew calm and sort of happy. It's boring out in the Asian waters sometimes, little winds most of the time, and even though a storm could have terrible characteristics, still it was a fight the men thought they deserved, just like sailors in warships who welcome the battles.

After a bit we all felt a nice fresh wind in our faces, and saw the dead surface of the water ripple up, and a few skites of spray dash from the ridges. We had just one sail up, on the main mast, and were soon moving across wind with a healthy surge, the steersman keeping firm at the wheel. The wind stiffened, and began to feel like wood, and the sailors looked over at the Captain, wondering if he minded. Suddenly the Captain was all orders, shorten the sail there, bring up this and that, and the crew were like monkeys again, over the rigging. The stronger the wind got, the less sail the Captain showed, till we were on the last acre as they say, and the rigging-men came down. The sea was different now, full of movement, and the ship was wallowing slightly in the commotion. Many of the crew went down to their bunks, because they weren't needed, and there would be work for them all through the day, and they would be better fresh up.

For about two hours we weathered the first lip of the storm, and for a time it looked like we had seen the worst of it. The sea was pretty bad, with fifteen foot waves, about the size of three men standing on top of each other. The sail up above was full to bursting, and sometimes it rattled so loud I thought Tom the Raven was shooting at me from the crow's-nest. When the ship began to roll like a fat dance, the Raven came down from his nest and gave me such a crack on the cheek with the back of his hand that it took me a good half hour to cheer up again after it. The red sky was gone, there were only charcoal-black clouds racing up the heavens, pouring over our heads like smoke. The sea changed colour, to a gloomy pitch, and even the spray being tossed up looked dirty and angry. It seemed like we had switched from the quiet mysterious Asian Sea to some filthy dangerous spot on the English coast. I went down myself to my bunk, but I couldn't rest. I could see the crew lying in the dark on their beds, blankets thrown over them, their boots still on if they had boots, or big bare feet well-calloused like the Captain's poking out over the edges. I knew that the Captain had picked them well, because the main part of the crew were asleep. They had seen like weather before, and judged they must be fit for the job ahead.

I was too restless myself, and went back up across the deck, moving with care from hand-hold to hand-hold, to go down to the hold. The paying-passengers were out in the corridor, being knocked about in a group, and they seemed to be choosing one of their number to go up on deck. They were all wearing expensive-looking clothes, with gold cuff-links in their sleeves, and one man was mopping his forehead time and again with a silk handkerchief, and saying:

'Mein Gott. Mein Gott.'

When they saw me, they rushed at me like dogs, and started to ask me questions in all sorts of languages, German, Spanish, Portuguese. The only English-speaking man among them, a small quiet man with spectacles on his nose, kept to the back of them, and could only half-raise his hand to get their attention before the force of their babble discouraged him. I told them that they had best keep to their cabins, strap themselves into their bunks, and not budge. This the Englishman managed to get translated to everyone's satisfaction, and it was surprising how relieved they all were to get a bit of advice, even from a twelve-year-old cabin-boy. They lurched and stumbled back into their cabins, the Englishman clutching with one hand onto his glasses, and I went on to the hold. It was hard going, because the ship was in a heavy roll, and you had to have a bit of experience I think to be walking about that day.

The horses were already in a state, snorting and neighing in a lather of suspicion. They were stamping about on the wooden boards, as if they wanted to discipline the ground into staying flat and still. The Muleteer, who had slept with them now for about two days, and was in love with them, was almost in tears, rushing about even against their hindquarters, trying to soothe them, and making sure they were tied fast. I waved to him, and he waved back, sort of grateful he wasn't being forgotten. The Captain appeared from the door at the other end of the hold, and he and the Muleteer had a hurried talk. The Captain liked always to be on deck, but he understood the horses, and he had as much concern for them as he had for the crew.

On deck the sea was a sight. It had somehow grown to

40

a larger scale than the ship. There were waves like hills coming at us at a slant, and every time the nose of our ship bit into one, you thought we were going to tunnel in there and be swamped. Each time the old ship heaved herself up the wave, dragging her timbers behind her, and we crested the great wave and sped down the other side. At the other side of every wave of course there was another mountain to climb, and the exact same effort for the ship to make. We were taking lakes of water at each trial, because, though the ship brought us up, she could never manage it before a flood of water had washed her foredeck. No one was forward now, it was impossible to stand there with the sweep of the sea. A contingent of the crew were manning the pumps at the back of the ship, two men to each handle, working away at them up and down. The nose was so great that the sound of their efforts was drowned, and the usual mutter of the pumps, that rush of water that sounds like safety itself, couldn't be heard. They were naked to their leather belts, and their bodies, some thin, some muscled, were all striving with the same purpose. The wind and the sea boiled around them, and their legs were in water at every wave. Each half hour four new men came up and the others went below and rested, because it was hard work. The Captain and Top Harry, standing beside the steersman, were the only ones besides myself and the passengers who were spared the ordeal.

Before the Captain could do anything to save it, the wind got into the sail we were showing, and started to tear it. It only ripped it here and there, because our sailmaker was a good one, and the Captain began to worry for the mast. We needed some pull besides the rudder to keep the ship heading into the waves, but that sail up there was filled fit to bring the mast down.

'Bring up the dredge-sail, Harry!' the Captain roared. 'We'll put it behind!'

Top Harry sent a man down for the dredge-sail. That

was a thing like a big kite you could throw in by a rope behind the ship, and it kept you safe into the waves. It was only used in the worst emergencies, because usually a little sail aloft and the rudder would be enough. I saw the man drag it up with another of the crew, and they tied the rope firmly to the bollard aft. Just then the wind worked up worse, and the Captain's attention was diverted to the main mast. He cried something out to Top Harry that the wind whipped away and I didn't hear, and Top Harry started forward immediately. He sprang for a ladder of the mast and my heart fled up into my mouth as I watched him grapple his way to the top. That's how he got his name, Top Harry, for being an expert in high seas at doing difficult 'top' work. But I doubt if even he had seen such a storm before, with the ship pitching the mast about at sixty degrees, and the whole Asian Sea coming over the decks at me and the Captain and the men at the pumps. It was the noise the storm made too, that continuous bellowing and roaring in your ears, like a rude and nasty policeman, that made your legs feel so weak.

Top Harry reached the highest spar and was starting to cut away the sail. There was no chance he could tie it in, and anyway when the hurricane died away we could bring up any number of spare sails. He started to cut, and at each cut the wind seemed to grow more savage, bulging the sail. You could see the canvas lashing against Top Harry, trying to slap him unconscious. The Captain stared up at his mate, without blinking in the vicious wind, his big hand grasping a deck-hold. There was a sudden crack, and the great mast started to split at the base, three or four feet up from the deck. The Captain never moved. He knew what the sea was going to do, and he knew Top Harry knew. I could almost hear the ropes beginning to snap, the thick American ropes we had got in Borneo. The mast keeled, keeled, came over a few inches, and Top Harry was suddenly coming down the ropes like a huge fairy. He had cut away the last of the sail, and here

42

"The mast keeled…"

he was now, trying to get himself back to safety. The mast came down like a railway barrier, and struck the rail of the ship, ripping itself up, in a tangle of ropes, from the centre of the deck. It leaned far out into the sea, pulling us over, and giving the ship an awkward roll. The Captain had men over at it immediately, cutting the ropes. A tall man I liked, a mute, had an axe and was hacking away at the last of the joining wood. The men jumped clear as the whole tree slipped further and further from its roots, and launched itself into the water. The ship was starting to swing broadside against the waves, the steersman frantic at the wheel to hold the pull. The Captain almost screamed for the dredge-sail to go over aft, and I saw the men haul the contraption over. In a minute the ship pulled straight, and though we were not safe, we were in a better condition to survive. We never saw Top Harry again.

There was a hole ripped in the deck above the hold, and water was going down there like a spring river. Men were trying to get something over it, because even above the noise of the hurricane, we could hear the horses below crying and screaming in despair. The pumps were being worked tenfold harder, because of the added sea in the hold, and there was a new desperate air in the men's faces, and only the Captain stayed firm because that was his job. He had lost his mast, a sorrowful thing for a weathered ship, and worse than that he had lost a long-time friend and mate in Top Harry. He stood there by the wheel, keeping an eye on the steersman who was now strapped to it, and looked much the same as always.

I struggled down to the hold to see what was up. The Muleteer was to his waist in water, and the mares were being crashed and battered about. They had horrible bruises on their flanks from being continually knocked against the stalls, and the Muleteer was doing his best to get sacks tied around them to protect them. The real problem was the stallion, who was rearing and biting at his ropes, lashing out at everything. He was so agitated you'd think there were a hundred pitchforks being driven into him. The Muleteer could do nothing except try and pat the horse's neck, but the animal was a long way beyond being able to hear, and was in a pure panic. Suddenly he wrenched himself loose, and the Muleteer made a lunge for the halter. Whatever the stallion intended by getting free, the pitch of the ship soon made nothing of it, and started to fling the horse about the hold. The mares in fright kicked out at him, and I had to close my eyes. The horse tried to drag himself to his feet every time the ship paused at the height of its roll, but each second after he was being knocked again into some other corner. The Muleteer, not caring now for his own life, leaped for the stallion and put a sack around his head. It was an extraordinary thing to see so little a man fell the horse like a cowboy with a bull. He lay on the horse's neck, the water pouring down both their throats, and by some magic effort, using all the help of the ship's evil roll, he half-floated the stallion in a surge of sea-water into his stall. Even before the stallion struggled to his feet the Muleteer had him tied in at least three halters. And suddenly the rolling of the ship stopped, or at least calmed, and using that miracle, the Muleteer made safe the stallion, and checked him for broken bones. The horse was still in a mad state, but when the Muleteer saw me watching from the door of the hold, he gave me an insane and happy smile.

I raced back up on deck to see why the ship had stopped rolling. All the way I was rejoicing at the thought of the storm being over, and I came out on deck almost laughing. The sun was in the sky again, and the wind was only stiff and no more. But the Captain and the men were standing like statues, with none of the joy of victory. It occurred to me that the storm had stopped a bit too suddenly.

Out about a mile in front of us there was a long high

island. There was something very smooth and unlike the Asian islands about it. It was a tidal wave.

The men were dripping with water and sweat, red and weary in their faces. They couldn't believe their bad luck. The Captain started to breeze orders at them to make them wake up. He had another dredge-sail brought on deck and tossed over the back. There was nothing for it but point the prow at the wave and hope the old ship could drag us over. The little Englishman, smiling, put his head out on deck, and was about to say something about the improved weather, when he saw the tidal wave in front of us, and ducked his head back and disappeared. Out of sight, out of mind. The Captain and I and the steersman, after the crew had been sent below and the hatches battened, crept into what they call the hurricane-house betweendecks, which was a small stout little place I'd never been in before. We had a thick glass window to look out of, and I think we were all quite thankful that there wasn't a perfect view through it. The wheel had been lashed firmly, and the dredge-sails were keeping us true.

The wave was almost silent, or it had a noise that wasn't anything to do with life, a sort of high-pitched noise that cut your ears like a blade. It was like being an ant before a human, because the wave was so big you couldn't really see it. It filled everything.

When it hit the ship we simply disappeared. It seemed likely we had gone in and were now being twisted and dashed to the bottom. We were only a shell of timbers, we couldn't expect the ship to make it. The three of us were crushed back against the door, and we were either going up very quickly or down like a boulder. The spray was everywhere, the movement so fast that the sea didn't have time to get in at us solidly. Why the little house wasn't ripped from the deck I don't know. We burst upwards, and saw a great belt of sky, and someone it seemed had exploded a hundred cannon-balls of water, because the air was made of pure white spray all around us. And then we were rushing down the other side of the wave.

Everyone felt mad in the head for a bit I think. It had been too much for me anyway, and I lay there in the hurricane-house a long while after the Captain had picked himself up to inspect the damage.

I went out and found everything stripped from the deck, the two smaller masts, the wheel, the cookhouse, and my poor bucket and brush with them. Only the two ropes, slacker now, were trailing out behind, the one piece of luck that had kept good. I began to cry, because it was then I fully realised that old Top Harry was gone. The Captain came over and put his hand on my back, patting it.

The island he had been aiming for was on the horizon, a biggish place with a tall mountain in the centre. He had the long-boat raised up from the small hold, and a crew of eight began to tow us towards the land. There would be survivors from the wave there, people who had reached the safety of the high ground. I went down the worn stairs to see the horses, and stepped with my school-bag from the evening train.

V MISTER CREEK'S SECRET

SOME MORNINGS are sad. It's not that it's raining, but there's a slaty sky above the bay, and the sea-gulls have no wind to soar on.

I sat on my bag, by the bus-stop, and tried to lean against the wall comfortably. Each way I turned there was a quirk of stone sticking in me. That woman, the one I told you about, it was irritation to see her pop her pony-tail in and out of the door – such a pointless thing to be watching at my age. I put my head between my knees.

I raised my eyes, and was looking at an unkempt garden. A high wall was at the end of it, with rusted gates. There were weeds in the 'flower-beds', and the wall was caked in soot. My school-bag had disappeared underneath me, and a worn lintel was there instead.

A carriage spindled in the gates and up the gravel, and swung in front of me, and stopped with a tremble.

'Oh bother bother,' said a voice from inside the vehicle, and a long foot, or rather a long shoe, put itself out on the top step. The foot was followed by a plump leg in silk stockings, and then a plumper thigh – much plumper.

'Oh strain and strumpet!' the voice whined.

A stick flourished into the open, grasped by a petulant hand. From the gloom emerged a belly like a pumpkin, dressed in a yellow waistcoat, and a pair of shoulders. The clothes were just too small, though smart enough in a greasy way. The little head wore a top hat, which some-one at some time or other had sat on. The face was squashed too, with the nose falling down on the mouth, and the eyes, tiny eyes, barely open under the flesh of the brows.

He surged towards me, his thighs having trouble avoid-ing each other.

'Up, Belemus, up! Back to the Room! I've work for 'ee this day!'

I jumped up and stepped aside. He bungled away

48

through a door inside the hall. An old shadow like a mouse came forward and whispered in my ear:

'That Mister Creek be an old humbug, he be,' she muttered. 'Should be butchered orf, by Gord.'

I went along the hall till I reached a stairway. A smell sidled down it, and I thought twice about going up. But I had to. I stepped up the creaky boards, and round some bundles lying on the ledges. Small snores were coming from them. They were babies.

In the Room at the top were groups of women and men and children. I passed scores of beds with gloomy rags resting on them. A sign was hanging from the middle of the ceiling:

MEN WOMEN AND CHILDREN SEPARATE
NO CONTACT
NO GODLESSNESS
Signed:
Missis Creek

I headed across the floor to where the children were.

'What you want to go sneakin' abou' fur?' a boy said to me. 'Want uz all knackered?'

'They won't box us young ones yet, Mimmer,' I said. 'Too much work in us.'

'Aye,' said a narrow boy, 'but they moight box jus' one uv uz fur t'example uv it.'

A thin light like gruel was coming down on top of them from the windows above. An arm here and there was lain over a pair of eyes or hanging down from a mattress. The healthier ones like Mimmer and the narrow boy were sitting in a bunch on one of the beds, smoking.

Mister Creek's wife strode up like a spear and lined us in a row – those of us who could stand. The others were put in their wheelchairs, and we pushed them to the Eating-room.

" "That Mr Creek be an old humbug, he be," she muttered,
"should be butchered orf, by Gord"'"

As soon as we were all in the lock was turned, and we sat at the rough table. Missis Creek unhasped a latch, and bowls of soup were passed through to her from mysterious kitchens beyond.

'No eating till I say,' she hissed.

We passed the bowls around the table, till the twenty of us had steam rising to our noses. Missis Creek brought her cane out from under her apron. She had her smile on her lips, watching us, watching us.

'Think of God, children! Think of the agony in stony places! Think of the fasting and the slow dying, and you too shall be as little lambs at His feet!'

This was a signal to eat, and just in case it wasn't, we all took up our spoons at the same time, and fell to.

Just as I finished, Mister Creek bumbled in the door, rattling his keys.

'Duck,' he said, 'will 'ee ever come on. It is already after ten.'

I scraped up from the table, and not glancing at my friends in case Missis Creek kept me back for it, I went out after the Beadle through the dormitory. We clattered down the stairs past the sleeping infants, and into the city air.

'You ride where you belong, Duck,' Mister Creek called to me, as he laboured into the carriage.

I crawled underneath the chassis and sat astride the front axle, and clung to the high bolts on either side. The coachman laughed when he saw me disappear.

We set off through the cobbled streets of the city, the coach swaying and shaking, and the hooves of the old brown horse skiting up sparks and stones. I preferred the sparks – they vanished before they hit me. Whenever the coachman could he took a corner quickly – though Mister Creek squeaked in protest – because that way there was the chance I'd be dislodged. It wasn't easy keeping a balance, with the cobbles rushing a few inches under my bottom, making me dizzy.

We hit on unsurfaced streets, and these gave way to a single highway into the country. I couldn't get a clear view of anything, just the shoes of people, and the clutter of rubbish and old bones in the gutters.

We bounced on through what I guessed were green fields. I saw ditches and hedges and trees when the springs of the coach flung us in the air. I could hear Mister Creek all the time, mumbling and complaining, telling the coachman to hurry, to slow down, not to bump, and now and again in his confusion, to bump. But the coachman sailed on regardless of all commands.

We slowed, and I heard Mister Creek open the carriage door and lean out.

'Come up, Duck, come up,' he said, and I slipped out, rubbing my bruises, and stood on the dusty road. We were drawn in at a pair of gates, painted black with gold on top, and inside the railings there was a place with carved wood under the eaves of the roof.

'Get in with me, Belemus, there's the lad,' Mister Creek said.

I climbed up into the leathery carriage, and slid onto the warm seat beside the Beadle.

'No, no, ye pesty orphan, not too close, not too close!' Mister Creek squawked, brushing me away from his clothes as if I were a ravenous moth.

I pushed over into the far side of the seat, and Mister Creek called out to the lodge:

'Hoi! Gateman! Throw your portals for the Beadle!'

A man with two barefoot kids behind him came running from the door of the house. I suppose he thought he might be facing the Beadle in different circumstances one day, and it would be as well to humour him now.

'Comin', yer Honour,' the man mumbled out, 'sher I wasn't 'spectin' you this day at all.'

'Will 'ee hurry, man,' said the Beadle, with all the deepness he could encourage in his voice, 'I've an appointment with his Lordship.'

'Certainly, certainly. His Lordship, is it?'

The lodge-keeper turned his big key in the gate, and swung it open. The coach swept in, and we sped along a flat road into the estate. I hadn't been there before, so it was all a new pleasure to see the fresh green spaces, and the old old trees standing quietly here and there, and a herd of deer racing across the turf away from us. The brown horse brightened a lot, because it was here he had spent his youth, and I could hear a new click click click in his hooves that sent a thrill through me. The coachman didn't understand the horse at all, and was saying:

'Pull up there, pull up.'

But it wasn't any good, the old fellow knew he was home.

We began to ride on a slight incline of the ground, and around a long line of trees we saw a place the size of the moon. There were two castle-like parts on each side of a broad mansion. As we approached I counted about fifty windows. The castley parts of the house were very old-looking, with high turrets, and autumn ivy and Virginia covering each inch of stone. Only the little and the big windows showed through. The central section, newer than the rest, was made of a soft brick, with tall windows, which got less and less tall as they moved up to the roof. There wasn't what you'd call a front door, but a huge pillared entrance, with four high columns supporting a pediment, and a flight of steps to the carriage-sweep in front. We clattered up, the old horse neighing, and about six dogs, shooting-dogs, and big water-dogs, came bounding around the side of the house to either greet or devour us.

I stepped out, because I was excited to see so many animals, and they rushed about me barking and jumping, and generally letting themselves go. It was almost as if they knew me. They soon quietened when a gentleman walked around the house after them. He smiled to see his dogs obedient, and I ducked to the other side of the carriage so I wouldn't be in the way. Mister Creek rumbled down from the coach, and gazed about short-sightedly for the owner of the voice that said:

'Simon! Good fellow! How are you!'

'Ah I'm not too bad sure, your Lordship, not too bad,' the Beadle said, bowing his head and simpering. The lord slapped him a bit on the back to get him over the simpering, which I could see he didn't admire, and the two walked up the steps to the entrance. The coachman whipped up the horse, and rolled the carriage away under an arch to the stables. I hoped the horse would meet as many of his old acquaintances as he wished.

I was left standing, unprotected by the coach, on the gravel, and all I could do was stare up at the windows. There was something familiar about the place, though I was certain I had never been here before. Especially the tall lower windows, quiet on the red walls, and the shadows inside of white pillars, and rich surfaces, and books. I was shaking my head at it, happy just to be standing there, when the Beadle stepped back out on the porch:

'Don't stand *there*, Duck, go round the back! You're here to help the gardener, not stand idle, boy!' And he went in again.

I was just going off when I caught a glimpse at a window of a girl, and a wizened face bobbing and tapping beside hers.

The gardener was a man with a white and blue face.

'Got this from old Napoleon!' he laughed. 'Bit o' powder in my pores!'

He'd been fighting nearby when a cannon-ball exploded at some battle or other in France. Before we started work he went in to the kitchens and came out with a pork pie and a mug of lemonade, which was just the think for the pork pie, or maybe it was the other way round. Then we set off up a shaded path, moving under the hanging branches with a wheelbarrow, and reached the metal gates of a garden. Inside there were flowers, little and big, and hedges in the shape of circles and triangles. The gardener and I went down on our knees, with cushions under them, and we weeded away for an hour before we rested. The gardener was pleased with me, because I had kept pace with him and hadn't minded the work. But then he didn't know what a difference a pork pie made.

I was just thinking what a fine thing it would be to spend the rest of my days weeding in the walled flower-garden, when a man in expensive livery came dashing through the open gate calling for the gardener:

'Top Harry! Top Harry!'

It gave me a start to hear the familiar name, and when I looked closer I saw it was indeed the old mate, Top Harry, though much older and different looking in his gardener's weeds. But I was pleased that the storm hadn't been quite the end of him, and that he was alive here still in another world. I knew it was another world because *I* was the same age, and he didn't recognise me at all.

The footman tore up, and clutched my arm.

'Come on, you,' he said, 'there's a to-do in the house that needs a little 'un.'

Top Harry laughed and said:

'The house is the place for him alright, isn't he the spit of his Lordship anyway!'

'Get away with you, Harry,' the footman said. 'He's not coming in for to sip tea, anyway.'

I was pulled and bundled up the path and in through a back door, even though I could have much easier ran on beside him if the footman had just paused to let me tell him. Upstairs and downstairs we seemed to go, through dark passages and through big bright passages, past snug small rooms and huge lazy ones, till we came bursting at last out onto a long gallery on one of the upper floors. The room ran the length of the new house, and there were portraits of the lord's forebears in niches. A door towards the middle of the gallery was open. The high chatter and crying of a girl mingled with the deeper tones of the lord and Mister Creek, though Mister Creek was a good second to the pitch of the girl.

As we passed the portraits, unusual smiling ones, and stern sad ones, I felt the oily eyes watching me, wondering who I was, so ragged, running along with the footman through their handsome house. The pictures of the women especially, there was something about them, and one in particular, a recent-looking affair, with a young lady standing by a stallion. But we were by so quick I had barely time to be puzzled.

In the room was the girl I had seen at the window. The lord was there too, and Mister Creek, who was fussing and muddling about like a mad hen. In behind the footman and me came a lady in a blue dress, with a very straight back. When she heard that the fuss was only for her daughter's monkey, that had vanished up the chimney, she got angry and sarcastic, and made her husband laugh.

'I raced up here for the fun of a funeral,' she said, 'and you sensible people are gathered to rescue a monkey.'

'Well since we are here on behalf of the monkey,' said the lord, 'we might as well do the job, or Milly won't stop crying till supper-time.'

'And what do you propose?' said her Ladyship.

'My Lady,' said Mister Creek, 'I took the liberty of suggesting the insertion of my boy here into the – if I may be indelicate – chimney. He can then, by dint of his experience of the chimney-sweeping trade, carry the monkey back to safety.'

'Now what is indelicate about a chimney, Simon?' his Lordship said, a little beside the point.

Her Ladyship looked me over.

'This boy?' she said. 'Why, he's much too large.'

'His best years are, it is true, behind him,' said Mister Creek. 'But I assure you he can still manage wonderful big chimneys like as you have here, my Lady.'

'I don't mind,' I said, and they were all so surprised or shocked that I should have talked among *them*, that even the girl stopped crying.

'Oh, mother,' she said, 'whip him for being bold!'

I was pretty fond of the girl straight away.

'You don't mind, do you not?' said her Ladyship. 'Well in that case, Simon, send him up!'

I moved over the soft red carpet before Mister Creek could spoil the effect by giving an order, and pulled myself up the first feet of the chimney. There were the same hand-holds and foot-holds I was used to from the time I was five and doing this sort of work for Mister Creek. I was glad the bricks were cold, because heat blisters are a trouble afterwards. I climbed nearly twenty feet before I reached a place where the chimney narrowed.

'Going up!' I shouted below, like we used to, so Mister Creek or the sweep would know to send a smaller boy up if I stuck. This time if I stuck I stuck, and the crows would be able to nest happily on a permanently blocked chimney. I squeezed on up, getting, I suppose, awfully dirty, and kept on yard after yard till I saw above me a square of daylight. At that point you can see how slanty and irregular they make chimneys – the insides turn this way and that like the wall of a pier at the seaside. I kept getting caught by the hips or the shoulders, and I was soon scraped and bruised through the cotton of my clothes. I came out onto the roof, and the monkey was waiting for me, or seemed to be, a few feet away on the slates. The slates themselves sloped to the edge of the roof, and the air pitched away, four or five stories to the gravel drive.

I've found that animals are wary of me if they haven't met me before, but usually if I wait they'll come and investigate me sooner or later. I sat there hoping the same thing applied to monkeys as it does to dogs and cats and horses in a field. I don't know if they were all getting impatient in the room below, but their talk by the time it reached me was a kind of garbled ghost-babble, and I was spared having to obey their orders, if they were giving them. After half an hour the little animal couldn't bear it any more, and came over quickly to me and jumped into my arms. I liked him, and since the girl had suggested I be whipped just a while ago, I was full of plans to live secretly on the roof with the monkey and never be seen again. But I slipped him into my shirt anyway, and buttoned it, and climbed back into the chimney. I must have been careless, because I started to slide, and all I could do was keep the monkey safe on my stomach and let my back take the worst. I came to a stop in a severe crook of the chimney, and thought for a second that my hip was going to make me pass out I had hit it so hard.

I struggled on down, and reached the place where the chimney broadened. Again, from automatic memory, I called:

'Soot-ho!'

even though, strictly speaking, I wasn't cleaning the chimney, or meant to be anyway.

The monkey kept good and quiet in my shirt, and perhaps the darkness of the chimney soothed him. I climbed down the holds in the stone, with a pain at the top of my right leg, and my skin burning. When I hopped out onto the broad fireplace, they all stepped back without thinking from the piece of charred wood I must have looked like. I unbuttoned my shirt, keeping a hold on the monkey's leash, and the girl came over and gingerly took him from my hands, dirty though he was. Her Ladyship and his Lordship and Mister Creek and even the footman were laughing and patting the girl, and the footman went off to fetch something to get the animal clean with, and I stayed put on the fireplace not liking to shake more soot than there was on the carpet. When I moved my head, a cloud of black dust fell all about me. There wasn't any colour left on me except black, and the trickles of bright blood mingling with it here and there.

"I fell forward and everything passed out of my reckoning"

'Well,' said her Ladyship, 'we'll give your boy a good scrubbing, Simon,' she said to Mister Creek, ' and then he can skip on back to Top Harry in the garden. And we'll send him home with a penny for his efforts.'

She smiled at me, pleased with her good ideas, and I wanted to smile too, even though Mister Creek would have that penny for himself whatever happened, but before I could do anything else I fell forward and everything passed out of my reckoning.

I woke up in a soft high bed, with cool linen sheets and a low light in a little room. I thought I had never been so easeful before, though my back and hip were like lying on coals. Maybe I had dreamed of places like that in the workhouse, I can't remember. There was a woman in a lacy black dress smoothing my forehead with a cloth, and smiling at me as if she were fitting in every smile I needed before the wounds did for me and I passed away. All I could say was:

'Am I dying?'

She laughed. I swear I couldn't have cared much either way because it was so nice there and the workhouse was waiting for me if I recovered. I didn't mind, as I say, but she said:

'Och, mo stór, you'll see another summer yet.'

Now that did cheer me up, none the less, because I like summer, workhouse or not.

A while later her Ladyship came in with her daughter and the monkey, and all three of them looked at me timidly, as if they thought that somehow or other they'd done something wrong.

'Ma'am,' said the old servant, the gentle woman, 'I've a curiosity here to show.'

She lifted my right arm from the sheet, and rested it on the covers.

'I noticed it when I was washing the lad,' she said, 'a very curious thing. It was quite a shock, your Ladyship.'

Just below the elbow there was a scar I'd never seen before, or ever saw since, a scrap of a thing in the shape of a crown. Her Ladyship seemed to get a fright, and hurried out of the room, and returned a few minutes later with Mister Creek and the lord.

'...I tell you,' she said, as she swished back into the room, 'Nanny saw it first. I couldn't believe my eyes.'

His Lordship came over and looked at the crown, and thought for a bit. He looked up at Mister Creek, and Mister Creek was stepping back and forward on his long feet, and grimacing his already grimacing face. He kept saying:

'Ha, ha,' very softly, and making small waves of his hand.

'Simon,' said his Lordship, 'what is the meaning of this crown on the boy? Are we not the only family with such a mark? Are there other, perhaps humbler families, with the same device?

'Oh, heh,' said Mister Creek, 'there might well be, but, ha ha, not in my experience.'

Mister Creek broke into a sort of dance.

'Then what is this mystery?' said her Ladyship. 'Explain, man, if you can!'

'Your Lordship,' said Mister Creek, 'this wee lad, oh this bonny well-fed little scrap, is your sister's boy.'

'My sister?' said his Lordship. 'Don't be an ass, man. My sister married a small farmer and hasn't been in touch with me for years.'

'Yes,' said Mister Creek, trembling, 'she did marry John Kirwan as it happens, but his horse killed him. She came to me one night out of nowhere, was afraid to face you, she said. Gave birth to this wee lad in the best room of the little house I had then, you remember, when I were your bailiff. But she died, sir, she died.'

His Lordship's face went still.

'I see,' said her Ladyship, sharp as pins. 'And soon after you set up a workhouse with your wife – bettering yourself, you called it.'

'Well, eh, just to make a clean break of it,' said Mister

Creek, and I believe he was glad to get it off his chest at last, 'your sister, my Lord, left me and the wife a sum of money to raise the boy here with, and we thought that a little establishment would be the best means, and so ...'

'You scoundrel, Creek!' his Lordship cried. 'You misused a sacred trust! But it's my fault too! She was afraid to come to me!'

I was lying there making plans to give everyone in the workhouse a big feast now that I seemed to own it, and was dreaming about weeding in the garden with Top Harry when I wasn't out riding with my uncle the lord or having fights with my cousin. I was thinking of the long days of summer, and the nights of winter by a big fire, and all that sort of thing, when I woke with a jerk with my finger on the doorbell of my house.

VI   THE LITTLE GODS

I HEARD my mother come downstairs, and cross the hall. She sang out a bar of a song and left it hanging. The kitchen door opened, and I knew in another five minutes everyone would be down and breakfast under way. I slipped asleep.

I jerked awake in the folds of a different blanket. It was red, with a navy blue stripe on the hem. I was surrounded by rows of men sleeping in similar bedclothes. We had no real beds and were lying on the ground. It was early in the morning, with a yellow tinge over a scatter of woods on a far hill. Behind me up the slope I heard a stamp and snort, and I craned around and saw a line of tethered horses. A sergeant moved among them, checking their hooves and bringing them water, talking softly. On another part of the camp I could see the cooks beginning to move, bringing out their pans with a rattle.

Two soldiers with cornets, or maybe bugles, came out
from the other side of a large tent, wiping water from
their faces, and took a stand among the rows of sleeping
men. They raised the cornets to their lips, and paused,
watching the sun make the first nudge above the hills.
They blew sweetly, a swift tarantara, and the men about
me stirred and mumbled, or sprang to their feet in strange
underwear. The camp was full of talk and murmurs, men
wandering, their eyes half-closed, to the water barrels and
washing with loud noises. My section of the camp was
donning a uniform of red cloth, and over their narrow
trousers they pulled high boots. I had a uniform like that
laid out at my side. I put it on. The shirt was white linen,
and the jacket buttoned slant-wise across my chest. There
was a black helmet, with an ostrich plume flaming from
the top, and I stuck it on my head.

Smoke was rising from the fires of the cooks, and I
could catch the sizzle of meat. The cavalry officers, the
men in my group, had no troops to look after, so they
were rather lying about, and taking their time over going
to breakfast. The sergeants were still watering and feeding
the horses behind us – we could hear the wickering.

Our senior men were dressed quickest and went off to
the large tent. Their spurs brushed through the grass,
ringing when they tipped a stone. The men clumped a bit
because their boots were not made for walking in, and the
clumsiness gave them a swagger as they went among the
dressing infantry. A corporal at the entrance of the tent
lifted the flap for them, and they ducked in.

I lined up with the other junior officers for breakfast,
no one talking much because that was considered the
thing to do. The cook was serving steaks and ale, and
some of the men were drinking as much of the second as
they could. The sun was up a way in the sky, and we ate
quickly. We were listening for the next call of the buglers.

Another tarantara pierced out, and we made the final

buckling to our uniforms as we climbed the hill to the horses.

I pulled my saddle from the bar and laid it up on my gray. He knew me well, and nuzzled my neck with hot breath when I bent down to pull round his girth. He needed a martingale to stop him tossing his head, but I left it out on a day like this. I liked the way his white mane shook.

The senior officers came out from the General's tent, having breakfasted, and the sergeants were standing by their horses to help them.

'Mount up!' called Major Aston, and we put our feet in our lengthened stirrups and up we went. I felt the hard cold leather of my saddle underneath me, and sat in a stiff and proper position. Major Aston led us off two by two across the little valley to the woods where the sun had risen, and we stopped there under cover of the first trees.

Our hill and the hill with our camp formed the two top sweeps of a large field, a place without hedges or trees. On the opposite side we could see the enemy army, their tents and their flags like toys. We saw the fingers of smoke from their breakfast fires, and the stirring of the men as they moved down to take up positions.

They formed two big squares of men, or rectangles, spread away from each other on the furthest corners of their ground. Their cavalry grouped behind, in the open, the steel helmets signalling in the sunlight. Our troups formed positions roughly matching the enemy, except that the infantry was in three groups, ranged in a triangle on the slope of the hill. There was a noise from the men for a bit, which was dying down.

Our general and his commanders rode out from the tents, and galloped towards our wood, and we noticed away in the distance a similar party of riders leave the enemy camp.

We remained like that for another quarter of an hour, and you could catch if you looked some of the infantry men drinking from hip-flasks. The General looked at his commanders with a special glance, and rode down with them among the regiments, giving a speech of encouragement. The same thing was happening across the hill, and we wondered what the French general was saying.

'Well, boys,' said Major Aston, 'it'll be a good fight today.'

'We're well matched,' said one of the helmeted riders. 'It won't be like the last time, even though we won.'

'Not like the last time,' someone echoed, leaning forward in his saddle.

Our horses shifted, jingling the tack, and the wind crept through the tree-trunks and played with the plumes of the helmets.

The General retired up the hill with his sergeant and his second-in-command, and there was a long pause before our buglers sounded. On the opposite slope of the field other notes called out, and we saw their right army come forward down the hill. Our smaller contingent at the front shifted, the whole mass of men going down the field in a measured march. Colonel Thomson was leading them at the front on horseback, urging his men with a waving arm, sword drawn.

The gap between the two bodies of infantry seemed big to start with, but it wouldn't have taken more than ten minutes, on your own, to cross the valley, strolling on a summer's day.

Soon there was no more than a hundred paces separating the lines, and our army closed its ranks, the foremost men bringing down their spears, and generally in the valley we heard the sound of swords being drawn. Detachments of musketry broke off to the right and left and began firing in two columns, loaders and firers, at the opposing army. We saw the first men on both sides fall, but the soldiers behind them marched on, the ranks pulling together to fill the gaps. Colonel Thomson's bugler sounded the charge, and the drummer-boys at the front, stepping along as if they were off to a picnic, played on in the same loud murmur of sticks and skin. Colonel Thomson and the enemy colonel swept past each other, and were the first to mingle with the infantries. The lines met with a clamour of shouts, of pain and bravado. The centre of the joined crowd became a jumble, the ordered lines behind spreading out in wings to reach the battling. Colonel Thomson struck right and left with his sword in the thick of the encounter. As far as we could make out the enemy colonel had fallen, and we were sorry to see him gone so soon.

Our general gave the order for the two remaining regiments to move down the field, to await the outcome of the encounter. There was still a commotion, but the numbers of men seemed less. It was hard to keep my eye on one pair of fighting men – the movement was far away, and another strip of colour soon distracted me. Out on the edges of the main block there were couples warring away, one of the two eventually winning and running back into the fray. It was a terrible sight in a way, but all our blood was up in the wood, and we were eager for the command to join in. Our horses caught the excitement even more than we did, and backed about and were difficult to manage.

By now the battle had been going on for an hour, and it was obvious the sides were well matched, and there was going to be no decisive victory from this first clashing. The General gave his sergeant the order for the main advance, and the man rode down to the section of buglers. They sounded the retreat, as did the enemy, and we saw the fighters below disengaging obediently and coming away. They left a large area of dead and dying men, a splash of red and blue and yellow and green. The buglers sounded again. This was our signal.

We poured out of the wood, the horses in a strict canter. As we passed our rear armies, we heard the

"They came bowling down the hill"

cornets giving them the order to move too, and as soon as we heard that Major Aston brought us into a charge. We were to skirt the standing armies in the valley below, and join with the fresh force of infantry on the left.

The enemy cavalry were, not for the only time that day, using the same strategy, and they came bowling down the hill in three long lines to meet us. We spread out likewise at full pelt, and I could feel Goliath under me pushing himself to the last stretch of his muscles. I was in the front line, and the blood raced inside me to feel the long charge we were making, and see the opposing horses and riders stream down at us at a tremendous gallop. We were going so fast down the slope that when we hit the inevitable rise at the bottom the horses were half checked and surged up in an odd way like the crashing of a wave. The enemy engaged with us just at that moment, so they had that advantage of force and balance. A rider hit me all askew, trying to cut my shoulder with his sword, but I ducked in the saddle to get my breath back, and turned my horse with a wild swing to meet him. I spurred Goliath forward and he smashed against the enemy horse with the fierceness of a beast, and I struck down at the French rider with a high stroke of my arm. My sword hit his helmet and glanced from the steel, but I left a deep dent there. Our horses swung this way and that, trying to keep close, but the French horse was rearing in fright, and I saw the animal had received a gash in his haunch that was crippling him. I nodded this to the Frenchman, who was in mid-blow against me, and when he looked down he wheeled away, whether to remount or find someone more heartless to fight I don't know.

All about me was a flashing of arms and a bitter sound of pain from wounded men, and the horrifying squeal that horses make when a blade has surprised them. Major Aston was fighting on my left, exchanging blows with his enemy counterpart, and I saw a French rider sweep from a victory to attack him from the side. I surged forward and blocked the foreigner's path, and by luck got my sword home. The man fell instantly, and I was ill to me feet. It made me dizzy, and I was tottering in my saddle, warding off the blows of men coming at me with fury. I fought on like this, and got a cut down my back whose seriousness I wasn't able to judge. The Major and about twenty others of us seemed to be in an isolated group, and we knew the enemy had got the best of us. Somehow or other though we broke through, maybe about thirty of us in all, and thundered on up the hill to engage with the rear army marching down to join with our infantry.

The cannon on both sides opened up with shocking explosions, and I felt a new tremble in Goliath beneath me. The enemy weren't firing at us, but at the advancing army behind us, but our own cannon was as usual falling all around us. A ball came down and knocked Johnny Glendinning's head clean off, but we carried on none the less and prayed for better luck ourselves.

We spread out as much as our meagre numbers would allow, and Major Aston sprung a surprise. Because of our reduced force he knew we would do little damage to the huge body of infantry, and he swung us away at the last moment, right in the teeth of their musket fire, which dropped two more of us, and led us on up the hill towards the cannon. We veered to the left so we wouldn't be riding through the very worst of the shot.

We saw the gunners drag round cannon to deal with us, and they started loading and firing and cleaning at astonishing speed. They were certainly first-rate men, and I trembled when I saw them in such good form. Our swords were drawn, and at every volley of the cannon, one of us fell forward, clutching at his saddle. Our horses didn't betray us for a moment, and kept going forward like bulls. I could hear nothing except the gallop of hooves, and the roar every minute of the guns. About ten of us reached the mouths of the cannon, and we jumped the whole clatter, men and metal. The thing I noticed as we got into the camp was the number of dogs that were barking and biting around us. There were contingents of musketry there, and we lost men in cleaning them up. We fought well, dashing here and there, and were after a while able to turn our attention to the cannon. We knocked out about ten guns, that is we drove off or engaged the gunners in swordfight. We would have done more, but a body of enemy cavalry, a reserve force, came thundering from a group of trees above their camp. Major Aston knew what was what, and we fled.

The silencing of half the guns at that time in the battle gave our infantry an advantage. The two fields of men had joined in one twisting mass behind us, and as we retreated we had to skirt the struggling fighters. Our men had got the edge, and were driving the enemy up the hill before them. Encouraged by this, our seven- or eight-strong remnant swung about, and we charged back up the hill to meet the reserve cavalry chasing us. We fought like little gods, though we were one man against ten, and I don't know if some of the enemy broke away, but in another hour there didn't seem to be many of the reserve left mounted. By now our infantry was almost the victor, and we saw French soldiers running up the hill here and there, throwing down their arms as they raced. Some of us wanted to chase them, but Major Aston, who is an honourable man above all, wouldn't let us, but it was hard to resist all the same. The enemy broke up in a general rout, and there were men stumbling away in every direction, heading for hill and copse as fast as weary limbs could carry them. We saw at the top of the enemy hill the French general moving about, wondering whether to stay or go. When his defeat was obvious, the French buglers played a retreat, and those of our men who were not battle-mad, let the defeated go.

Our army sent up a wonderful cheer when they saw the French running for it, and threw up helmets and hats. We too, though we had lost most of our horses and our comrades, cheered with the rest, swaying in our saddles but happy.

It was late afternoon, with a hot sun high in the heavens. The General cantered down to us, and thanked us simply for our courage, and praised us. The field was quiet, not a murmur, all of us impressed by what had happened, a bit awed by it. Then there was that gradual strange moving away from the scene of battle, and a low talking starting up, and some men going out to find and help the wounded, and carry them to camp. We, the remains of the cavalry, sat for a long time astride our horses, and watched. We felt too weary even to trot, to walk, we just sat there thinking. Major Aston, with a wound across his shoulder, started laughing to himself, and stopped.

There were many dead men from both sides left behind as the soldiers drifted to the camp. There would be singing and drinking and feasting that night when the fires were lit, but for the moment, and indeed, at the back of our heads, for ever, we felt a sorrow for the loss of many lives.

I noticed the General at the far side of the litter of dead soldiers, turning his horse's head here and there among the corpses, looking for officers maybe, or men he had liked for their special bravery. We watched him moving, a distant figure, the only living man among the dead, his helmet plucked down under his arm.

We followed Major Aston at a walk back to camp. The cooks were merry, calling out to everyone their congratulations. I swung my leg over the saddle to dismount, and stepped down into night-time in my room at home.

VII THE CAVE

I WAS sitting on the 7A bus as it bundled along the Booterstown road. There's a bird sanctuary between the road and the railway, and the sea's beyond the railway. The patch of acres is the one wild thing I pass going to school. I rise in my seat to catch a glimpse of a duck or a heron.

The bus jolted and I was knocked against the seat in front. The man there was about to swing round when he turned into a tree. I was alone with the tree unless you count four or five other oaks.

I sat in the rain and the tall grass. The sky was stormy. There were clouds tugging up from the mountains in the distance, and thunder not far off.

I walked to the middle of the meadow. The place lit up with a dash of lightning. I blinked. The thunder rattled. My eyes waited for the next flash. Down it came with a spring into the ground, and a burst of black smoke. The rain fell. The lightning jagged. One of the oaks went on fire. I sat on a lump of grass. The storm strolled on by me and faded in the country beyond.

The tree was burning, and the rain didn't stop it. In fact the rain stopped.

There was a hill nearby. I tramped over in the mud. I reached some rocks and found a path leading up. I passed a cave as I climbed, and a minute later another. I glanced in and the people inside glanced out. Then we stared at each other for a moment, like a cartoon.

There was a man and a woman in short furry trousers and two boys with wild hair. The boys grinned. The father fumbled about on the floor and picked up a stick. He shook it at me. I smiled. He grabbed the woman and stood her in front of him, and peered around her back.

'Jak's cave here!' he said. 'Jak's cave!'

'Of course,' I said.

The boys sauntered to the entrance and looked my clothes over.

72

"One of the oaks went on fire"

'Jak's cave!' the man insisted.

One of the boys lifted a stone from the floor and tapped it against my jumper.

Jak hauled himself up and led me in. He was crying.

Everyone sat close together because it was a little cold. After a while I went back to the copse I began at, and gathered an armful of branches. The oak was burning low. I bound up some twigs that had leaves and lit them. I stumbled back and ran into the cave. They almost trampled me trying to get out.

I threw the sticks in the centre and put the wood on top.

The boys returned and skipped around me:

'Wow. Wow. Wow,' they said.

The mother crept to the fire. She sat down on the old stone beside it. I saw her eyelids droop. Jak couldn't resist coming back. He walked up beside the flames. He touched the red flickers and roared.

He and his wife didn't need to sit so close anymore. The boys rolled in the dust.

The boys and I built a woodpile at the back. They wanted to throw everything on as soon as I brought it in. We couldn't stand in the cave after a bit, so they got tired of it, since the air outside seemed colder.

It began to get dark. The mother pulled a carcase from a covering of stones. She tugged strips off and handed them round.

I hooked mine on a stick and stuck it in the fire. They watched me from the corners of their eyes. The meat roasted and I let it cool a moment and started to eat.

I offered a piece to the mother. She touched it and drew back her fingers.

'Dead wood,' she said.

Jak knocked it out of my hand in a friendly way, and gave me a strip of the raw stuff. I put that in the flames too.

I handed the boys slivers, and holding their breath,

they swallowed it. They looked at their mother and rubbed their palms across their stomachs.

They thrust their own strips in and munched away, though sometimes the meat was raw and sometimes black.

The mother got the hang of it better. She judged how it should be by tasting it, and in the end Jak took bits from her.

They rose when they were finished and left the cave. I followed them over the rocks to a stream that trickled from the hill. They drank. The boys played, splashing about. I noticed the four of them shivering. They went downstream and washed their hands and faces, and we returned to the cocoon of the cave.

An hour later Jak was sitting with his head on his knees, groaning, and the mother too. The boys gave up wrestling on the floor and huddled in a corner. The cooked meat wasn't lying easy on their stomachs.

I stretched on the ground near them when they were recovered and ready to sleep. I lay most of the night awake, throwing a stick or two on the fire. The others snored, curled beside each other.

The sun came up. I slipped out and plucked a bundle of dry grass. I sat beside the river and weaved it together till I had a long strip.

Jak tumbled into the light with his spear, and ran off across the meadow.

I bent the strip of grass around and tied it up. I made a section of woven grass for a bottom, and I had a bucket. I dipped it in the water. It held for a while. The liquid was escaping through tiny holes. I looked on the riverside for clay. I smoothed some around the wickerwork and left the contraption on a rock.

In the cave the mother perched behind the boys and picked through their hair. When she caught something she squeezed it. She popped out to the river and cleaned her fingers.

I got a copy-book from my school-bag. I drew a horse. One of the boys took the pencil and did a man with a spear. It was no trouble to him. His brother made some deer, running and walking, and a bird with claws coming down on a hare. I drew them a horse and cart – they didn't seem to see it.

I'd taken the paper out to show them how to make wheels and the other things they were lacking. But they only saw what they knew. The cart might as well have been a collection of squiggles.

Jak came back with a deer on his shoulder.

I climbed down to the stream to fetch the bucket. The day's sun had baked it. I filled it and carried it up. They were happy to drink from it. Jak – as he always did in the river – washed his deery hands. I snatched the bucket before one of the boys could get his mouth to it.

We grouped around the fire. Jak was sniffing. As soon as I noticed him doing it, I saw they were all at it.

They began to sneeze. Moisture dripped from their eyes. The fire and the air outside were giving them colds.

I thought of the objects I could show them, that would make their lives comfortable. The trouble was the way things were going they'd be dead in a week.

I poured the contaminated water on the fire, and stepped on the bucket till it was grass and dust again. I scrambled down to the burnt tree. The fire was gone. I looked back at the stony hill. There was no sign of anyone looking to see me go. I began to walk – and was sitting down to dinner at home.

VIII   THE ROUNDABOUT WAY

I was walking through Trinity College. It's a roundabout way to school but I wanted to see if any flowers were up. They have trees in the grounds, and at a certain corner of the cricket pitch there's a place where the gardeners have lain down daffodils and crocuses. I passed among maples, searching the cut grass for the green tips. There wasn't one. It was the first day of spring.

Both the men and women students in Trinity College have long hair. They crawl along the edges of the paths. They don't talk to each other as they go by, in fact they usually look the other way. The morning time, which is the rush hour for every school, is the most deserted hour for Trinity.

But that's why I like it. Sometimes up by the New Library a family of swallows is swinging and sliding above the flagstones. They whistle, swallows – I think it's a whistle.

And they have a row of old red houses in Trinity, with gables at the top, where I suppose some of the students are still sleeping when I pass.

There is a body of men about the place who wear riding-hats. They might be policemen, but they might not. They cross Front Square with intent strides, and with looks of superiority on their faces.

There was an example of this type coming over the cobbles that morning. His coat with its tails was cluttering behind him. I stepped in among the arches of the Campanile, with an eye on the clock above the dining-hall. It was a quarter to nine. I would have to skip up Grafton Street, dash around Stephen's Green, and belt up Leeson Street if I was going to make it. My heart started to race with worry. The riding-hatted fellow was taking his time. He knew the student he was on his way to catch and lock up would still be lazily asleep.

He spotted me and shouted:

'Hey, what you doing there?'

I stepped out from the protection of the old stone and stood on the grass with a swing-chain between me and the danger.

'What you up to?' the man said. 'Get off the grass.'

His forceful way of speaking left me paralysed. I wanted to ask him to pause for a second and let my lungs start working again.

'There's only Fellows allowed on the grass, you,' he said. 'Hop it.'

'I am a fellow,' I said, delighted with the rule. The man was so used to everyone having long hair, he had forgotten what a real boy looked like.

'Get out of it!' he said, and drew his foot over the chain to get closer to me.

I ran back under the Campanile, and out on the cobbles of the square. I didn't have time to talk to him anyway. I headed for the front part of the university. There's an arch there where the gates are. They were open, and I could see the traffic pouring and stopping in the view beyond the wooden leaves.

'Tom, Tom!' the man shouted behind me. 'Stop him!'

I was under the arches now, and Tom came out from his cubby-hole to see what was up. I went past with a smile, and said:

'Morning!'

'Morning, sir,' he said.

As I pounded out onto the pavement of the city, I heard him call behind me:

'What's that you say, Seán?'

Poor old Seán. One boy less for his roasting pot.

I weaved among the crawling cars and reached Grafton Street. I dodged about among the office-workers. I was proud that I could move faster than they could. It made me different from them. I don't think they noticed me though.

I tripped on the curb as I was crossing the road to the gates of the Green, and I tumbled over and over. I got up and there was no one about any more.

I shrugged my shoulders at the silent city. I sat on a bollard by the gates and watched a sea-gull floating in the sky. You know the way they do. They catch a wave of wind and ride on it till they get fed up and slide off.

The bird swooped around. The pavement under me was dimpled and cold. There was a thin sun now the morning was older. Long rays of yellow light were falling from holes in the clouds, slanting on the rooves and into Grafton Street. The sea-gull came down to the pavement and flew through it.

There was no hole where the bird entered. Up he came again without a thought, and fled into the sky. I looked hard at the concrete. It was just the usual thing, it wasn't even transparent. I shifted on the bollard. Very interesting. An improvement on your everyday pavements.

A mustachioed shopkeeper came out from his door. He looked about him, and stretched, and wiped his lips. He scratched his bald head, slowly and thoughtfully. He sighed, and took a saw from his apron, and stepped close to a shaft of sun. He touched the saw against the light. He drew his arm back and forward. A few inches later he stopped, and slipped the blade back in his apron. He yawned, and tapped below the cut he had made, and a fragment of light fell with a tinkle to his feet. He picked it up and went into his shop.

I trailed over to his window. He was at the back of the shop on a step-ladder. He was hanging up the lump of sun. Perfectly sensible.

A car drove up Grafton Street with a whoosh. It was going to pass me by, but it halted. The flowers from its exhaust stopped falling out. A policeman burst from the door. He had a square hat on and was upset about something.

'Are you lost?' he said. 'Are you lost? Could you be

79

lost? Is anyone lost nowadays?'

'I'm not completely lost,' I said. 'I'm on my way to school.'

'You have my sympathy!' he cried. 'I wish I could drive you into the country instead. We could have a picnic! Oh I'd like a picnic today. It's going to be hot!'

'Is it?' I said. That was good news.

'But I'll be dust by lunch-time,' he said. 'I've had a good life though.'

'Oh dear,' I said.

'Yes, it's my number today,' he said. 'Three zillion two billion nine thousand one hundred and seventeen. Look,' he said.

He held out a ticket to me, with the number he had mentioned printed clearly on it in violet ink.

'So,' he said, waving his head back and forth. 'C'est la vie.'

'Is that French?' I asked. It sounded like it.

'If you're not lost,' said the policeman, '*I'd* better get lost. Eh? That's a joke.'

'It's rather funny,' I admitted. 'Do you know many jokes?'

'No, only the one. But I like it, singular though it is.'

He squeezed back into his car, and waved to me.

'Keep safe!' he said. 'Watch out for the Walkers!'

'The Walkers?' I said, but he was gone, the tulips and the crocuses and the daffodils flooding out of his exhaust.

When the flowers had lain on the road for a minute, they disappeared.

I strolled along the perimeter of the Green and down Kildare Street and came to the Dáil, which is a sort of House of Parliament. There were none of the usual guards in their places outside the gates. Cars were running in and out, strewing flowers everywhere. They didn't bother to pass each other in the narrow entrance. They ran straight through. But there weren't any crashes.

80

No one stopped me from walking in. The Museum was on one side of me and the National Library on the other. A dog nudged one of the pillars of the library, and the building fell down. The people in the cars burst into laughter. Everyone got out and rebuilt the library in the shape of an office-block. They were all delighted with it. It took them five minutes.

At the door of the parliament there were men buzzing in and out. I climbed some stairs and stepped out on a gallery overlooking the debating chamber. There was a robed man down there, calling out the name of each delegate as he stood, so you heard the name first and then the speech from the Member of Parliament, like this:

O'Hackett!

'Wil, gintemin, I don't wish to keep you this morning. It won't do, all this keepin' and delayin'. But it's been brought to moi notice, and 'tis a great concerun to me, that them rats on Dunleary Pier are gettin' a rough deal. Dey're livin' in pathetuc squalor in houses not fit for humins. I would like to knowo what, if anythin', de Dáil proposes to do 'bout it.'

O'Grady!

'The honourable gentleman has obviously had steak for breakfast and toast for tea. I took care of the rats myself last year, they're living in luxury. Raise the standard of living now on the Pier and you don't know where it'll stop. Maybe even the King of Dalkey will expect us to send him new cushions for his couch. Or at least new covers, anyway.'

Quinn!

'I think we'd best think twice about this. No, three times. Lookit it this way: if we start worryin' about rats we'll end up worryin' about humans.'

There was agreement at this, with a mumble of 'Hare, hare' sweeping the room.

O'Laughlin!

'There should be more scope for squirrels. I say squirrels should have more scope!'

Quinn!

'Squirrels, is it?'

O'Laughlin!

'Yis.'

Quinn!

'Ta hill wid squirrels!'

O'Grady!

'Gentlemen, Gentlemen, we have a guest in the house.'

All eyes stared up into the gallery. I waved. There was a deep silence, and they all smiled.

O'Grady!

'Howaya.'

Duck! (How did the robed man know my name?)

'I'm well, thank you.'

O'Grady!

'Spot on.'

I lifted my school-bag, and with a nod, retreated back down the stairs and across into the road. I wasn't ready for politics.

I went over to South Anne Street. I think that's the name, or it might be Wicklow Street. There was a lady walking with a basket. I looked at her idly. I was wondering if the robed man in the Dáil ever got a sore throat from calling out the names from one end of the day to the other. The woman came on towards me. She turned into a puff of smoke, and trailed into the air. Then she was an old woman again, with thin gray legs, walking as before. Then next second there was a wolfhound where she had been, and then her again. A puff of smoke, a gannet, a flagship, a rhinoceros, an old woman. All as she walked along Wicklow Street. Or is it South Anne Street?

I met a nice fellow at the corner of the road. He was dancing in the middle of Dawson Street, without a care in the world. He was doing his dance for the White Church. His eyes ran over the façade, and he leaped and whirled and paused in celebration.

His face was serious, very serious. At the end the bells of the church rang out, and he bowed.

'Hello,' he said to me. 'How's tricks?'

I shrugged my shoulders politely.

'If you be my friend,' he said, 'I'll teach you how to fly.'

'Oh well...' I said, a bit overcome. 'Of course I'll be your friend.'

He looked down the length of Dawson Street. There was a boy coming up the middle of the tar, whistling.

'On second thoughts,' said my friend.

He sat on the ground.

'See that boy?' he said.

'Uh huh.'

'See me?'

I looked at the empty space where he had been.

'No,' I said.

The whistling boy came up beside me.

'So it's you,' he said. 'My name's Theo. It's a nice morning isn't it? Do you have any money?'

'I haven't a cent,' I said. 'Theo.'

'Well you're Belemus, everyone knows that, what a laugh!'

'Okay,' I said.

I would have preferred to learn to fly instead of talking to this boy whom I didn't like that much.

'Listen,' said the boy, 'stop dreaming. Wake up. See life as it is. It's cruel. Wake up.'

I glanced at the boy's face, and frowned. I didn't understand him.

'Honestly,' he said, 'I'm not joking.'

He walked over to the front of the church.

'Honestly,' he said.

He walked up the wall:

'I wouldn't kid a kid like you.'

He went half-way up the church, his body sticking right out parallel to the ground.

'Flying is a bore,' he said. 'You need a soul to fly. Walking is the thing.'

He rushed down the wall at me, his mouth opening. Two sharp teeth stuck out over his lower lip. I held up my school-bag to stop him, and his mouth bit into the leather. He gave a growl. I skipped back. The next moment he was as he had been, standing beside me. It was hard to decide whether or not it had happened.

'So,' he said. 'C'est la vie.'

'Is that French?' I said.

Saying that reminded me of the policeman's warning: 'Watch out for the Walkers.'

'I have to be going now,' I said. 'I'm late for school.'

The boy looked at me oddly.

'You know what I am, don't you?' he said. He didn't move.

'I think so,' I admitted.

'Do you want to come along with me?' he said.

I looked at him, embarrassed.

'Do you want to?' he said.

There was something about the way he said it that made it hard to refuse. His mouth opened, in a smile, and for a moment at the ends of his fingers I saw a flash of claws.

'No, I don't,' I said. 'In fact, I don't at all.'

'Sure,' he drawled. 'Another time. See you around.'

He strolled up the street, and the other boy reappeared on the ground.

'That's what I call a narrow escape,' he said.

He jumped to his feet. He didn't mention flying again – I was sorry.

'Look,' he said, 'I'm hungry. Let's go to Bewley's and pick something to eat.'

I had a packed lunch in my school-bag. But I had about one and threepence in my pocket. I supposed it might buy a cake and a lemonade if I was lucky.

'Of course it will,' said the boy, though I hadn't supposed out loud. 'Don't worry about it. If your luck's bad, worrying won't change it.'

We went together along the side-road to the café. There was a smell of coffee in a flood outside the door, and a man behind the window pouring beans into a machine. The boy smiled to see the man and gave him a wave. The man seemed timid, and fed himself to the machine and hid from us.

We were brought to a table in the middle of the tea-room. There were a few other people about, reading. We sat at the glass-topped table.

'Wait here,' the boy said. 'I'll get a magazine.'

He went to the counter and brought one back. He opened it up. It was called Handy Household Hints. He paused at each advertisement, nodding his head, and saying:

'Maybe, I don't know. What do you think, Belemus?'

I gave a sort of turn of my hand to show I didn't know either.

He stopped for a longer time at a picture of a plate of cakes. There were two cups of coffee steaming beside them. The boy put out his hand and tapped the page.

'Good picture,' he said. 'Well drawn.'

'Yes,' I said.

'Okay,' he said. He reached his hand into the advertisement and brought out the plate of cakes.

'They're a little out of scale,' he said. 'But I'm not a perfectionist any more. There was a time when I wouldn't have touched crooked drawings.'

He took out the cups of coffee, and laid them on the table. They were crooked too, because of the perspective the artist had used to make them look real. And here they were, really real now, and looking a bit false.

'Hmm, they're good cakes,' the boy said, eating away. 'Fresh cream too,' he said, looking at the date on the

85

magazine. 'Well it would be, it's this week's. One thing about Bewley's, it never has old editions.'

I saw that the other customers were choosing their food too from what they were reading.

'Bewley's has changed a lot since I was here last,' I said.

'That so?' said my friend. 'When were you here?'

'Last Christmas with my grandfather. We went to the Walt Disney cartoons up the street.'

'Oh,' he said, 'The world doesn't hang about for the likes of us. On she goes, like a mad train. Everything changes, sooner or later.'

'I wish it wouldn't,' I said, and as I said that, it did change, and I was walking with O'Donnell out the school lane.

O'Donnell said:

'Sometimes, Belemus, you don't talk all day.'

IX   THE CASE OF THE STATELY BORZOI

THE first lesson next day was mathematics. We have an energetic mathematics' teacher. As soon as the bell goes he sweeps in, in his black soutane, and starts the lesson as if there were no time to be lost. The tornado technique.

X and Y sums are a puzzle to me. I suppose they're meant to be. But are they supposed to be so much a puzzle that I never get the answer? Sometimes my father gets it for me, but it's only *an* answer, and rarely *the* answer. So any hint of X and Y sends a chill over my heart. 'If you have seventeen oranges...' is a bad beginning, in my opinion, to a day's school.

'If you are a kennel owner,' the priest said, ' and you

have 302 dogs, and there are 7 thieves on the prowl looking to steal 36 dogs each, how many cats are there in
Barcelona?'

Well it was something like that, but I dodged the end of
it. Ugh. I didn't want to know. The priest was standing
with his jaw thrust forward, eager to find the answer to
this wonderful problem.

I bent down to get my jotter and a pencil. I had to
humour the fellow or he'd be down on me with his
enthusiasm. When I raised myself up the priest with his
equation had gone, and I was alone in a room.

No, not quite alone, there was a man in the corner next
to me. But he was so self-effacing that he almost wasn't
there.

'Oh hello,' he said. 'Didn't see you come in. Well done.'

'Eh, thanks,' I said.

The man shifted his legs, changing from one knee to
the other. I saw that the sole of his raised shoe was loose,
and hung down like a pancake from the leather upper.
His clothes were not new. I saw a line of yellow on the
edges of his cuffs. He swivelled his shiny jacket-sleeve
when he noticed me gazing at it, and he coughed.

'I'm you know, in disguise,' he said.

'Of course,' I said.

'I've been in disguise,' he said, laughing, 'ever since my
last job.'

I laughed with him.

'Oh well,' he said, 'our line of work has its ups and
downs.'

'It has,' I said.

There were two doors in the little ante-room. I noticed
this because a man in portly tweeds entered the first door
softly and walked in through the other door softlier. He
managed to say as he crossed our line of vision:

'Sorry, sorry I'm late.'

The man in his disguise gave me a look, making a

gesture with his lower lip. I raised an eyebrow to show him I agreed, whatever he meant. We heard rustling and the noise of a chair falling over in the next room, then:

'First please!'

I think it was first please he said, but it sounded like 'Fre'eze'.

'That's me, I think,' said the disguised man. 'Unless you were concealed here before me?'

'No, no,' I said.

So I was left on my own.

The top half of the first floor was made of glass. There was something written on it, like this:

OTTOIG YRNEH
evitceteD etavirP

It wasn't exactly like that – some of the letters were back to front too. I wondered if it was a code. I got up and opened the door, and on the other side was the same thing, the other way round:

HENRY GIOTTO
Private Detective

Ah, I thought.

I sat down again. I caught the mumble of voices in the next room. A little later there was a shout:

'But that case was lost, truly lost, Mister – what did you say your name was!!'

An apologetic rumbling went on for a bit, and the door opened. The ragged man was now disguised as a sad ragged man. He moved through the gloomy room, and didn't look at me. He opened the door and vanished into the difficult world outside.

'Next!'

I crossed to the door. Such a shouty man. He was sitting at a bare brown table as I came in. There were newspapers on the thinly carpeted floor. He had a tall old half-painted window, from which drifted a gurgle of traffic from below.

He was slumped in his chair, his shoulders in a bow. He was looking at a spot in space somewhere between us.

'I suppose you're some mad PD's assistant too. Well I've decided to become a baker, so you can go home.'

'Actually,' I said, 'I found myself here quite by chance.'

'You know,' he said, glancing up at me with interest, 'so did I. About fifty years ago though, but still.'

'I was finding school a bit boring' I explained, 'and here I am.'

'Good,' he said. 'Good, good, good. A trifle young maybe, but I was young too when I started. We're all small to begin with.'

'Are you offering me a job of some sort?' I said.

'Exactly,' he said. 'A job. Well, when one turns up, anyway.'

'Alright,' I said.

'Yes,' he said. 'I thought I'd hire an extra pair of eyes, just in case.'

'Just in case you get a case?'

'Precisely.'

'Alright,' I said.

'You can sit over there,' he said, pointing out a smaller desk, with a chair against it, one of the swivel sort. 'Yes,' he reminisced, 'I started at that desk, when the late lamented Jeremiah Giotto was still alive. My,' he said, 'father, you know.'

'Oh,' I said, 'I see.'

'Yes,' he said. 'Yes, yes.'

I took my place at his old desk. The chair needed oil, but it didn't fall apart. The old room was panelled in wood, and there was a clock in a glass case on the marble mantelpiece. The clock said a quarter to eleven.

It made a sound like this:

Tack, Tuck. Tack, tuck. Tack, tuck. Tack, tuck, and so on, till on the fifteenth stroke it said:

Tick, Tock!

I and Henry Giotto sat quietly, drumming our fingers on the wood of our desks. Now and then he sighed, a gentle tweedy sigh:

'Pofffffffffffff...'

'Poor business, this spring,' he commented.

'Oh?' I said.

'Yes,' he said.

We listened to the muddle of traffic passing beneath the window.

'Where is this?' I said.

'Hampstead.' He turned in his chair, mildly surprised.

'In London?'

'Why yes. Exactly.'

'Oh.'

There was a tap on the door beyond our door. I heard it like a small hammer. The tap became a rap when it wasn't getting any response.

'They usually work it out,' Henry Giotto said, nodding his head. There was a bald section right on top of it.

We heard the outer door open, as if someone were peeking their nose in.

'Anyone here? Cooee.'

'Ugh,' said Mister Giotto. 'What a vulgar expression. We must brace ourselves,' he warned, turning to me briefly.

'Anyone, I say, anyone at home?' said a woman's gravelly but high-toned voice.

'Yes, I say, yes there is!' Henry Giotto called out.

A large woman entered our door. She stared at us with her circular white face, one hand balanced on the handle. She was wearing a black dress with white lines all down it.

'Have I got, I say, have I got the right address?'

"Pardon me?"

'Whom are you looking for, my dear?' said Henry.

'Em, Goto, Mister, Private Detective.'

'Gi-ott-o, madam, that's I. Or me if you're not grammatical. This is my assistant Mister, Mister, eh...'

'Duck,' I said.

'Oh ho,' said the woman, 'how quaint. Duck. Ha ha.'

'And your own name?' said Henry.

'Constance Heather-Heather,' said the woman. '*Lady* Constance Heather-Heather,' she said.

'Is that the Heather-Heathers of Dorset?' asked Henry politely.

'No,' said Lady Constance sadly. 'Blackpool.'

'Never mind,' said Henry. 'Please take a seat, Lady Constance.'

She pressed herself into the newer swivel-chair in front of Henry Giotto's desk, and said:

'I'm in a terrible state. Oh terrible.'

'Please,' said Henry, 'take it from the top.'

'Pardon me?' said Lady Constance.

'Ah,' said Henry. 'Parlance of the recording studio. I was a, eh, singer in my younger days, on and off. Chiefly off. Off-key, anyway. I mean start at the beginning.'

'I was on my way home last night,' she said, drawing her ample legs together and leaning forward like a man, 'from a party at the Jackson-Walpoles, you know, the coal people, they have a house in...'

'Yes, yes,' said Henry, 'you were on your way home. What happened?'

'I, I,' said the woman. 'Oh dear, yes, Thomas turned the car in the gates, and the first thing I noticed was the silence. When we turn in the gates onto the drive there's usually a faint sound in the distance of Dolly barking. I open the window to hear it. Since my husband died,' she said, 'Dolly's been my only companion.'

There was an odd squeaking sound that Henry and I took to be crying. It came somewhere from the woman at any rate.

'So,' said Henry, leaning back and tipping the ends of his fingers together, 'your husband's been murdered, has he?'

I was startled.

'No, no!' said Lady Constance. 'Why ever do you suppose that? He died ten years ago!'

'Calm yourself,' said Henry. 'It was just a bizarre joke. I have an uncommon taste for the bizarre.'

'Well you gave me a little shock,' said the woman.

'Forgive me,' said Henry.

'Oh I do,' she said.

'Now,' said Henry, 'am I right in supposing that Thomas – I deduce that Thomas is the chauffeur – is blackmailing you? He has those love-letters between you and Mister Jackson-Walpole, perhaps?'

'Mister Walpole was an officer in Africa!' said Lady Constance.

'Come, come,' said Henry, 'we mustn't be prejudiced.'

'No,' said the woman. 'It's Dolly, Mister Giotto, it's Dolly that's been murdered!'

'Your dog?' said Henry.

'Or kidnapped,' said Lady Constance. 'If not murdered, kidnapped, the poor wee lass.'

'What breed is this poor wee lass?' said Henry Giotto. 'If you can hear her barking from the gates, you have either a very short drive or a very large dog.'

'The second is the case, of course,' said Lady Constance, offended. 'Dolly is a pure-bred borzoi.'

'Naturally, Lady Constance,' said Henry, throwing his eyes to heaven. 'Naturally you would have a borzoi.'

'Now I've heard among some of my, well, poorer friends, that you are the best criminal detective in the business,' said Lady Constance. 'I have come to you to appeal for help.'

'I'm very busy,' said Henry. 'It's been a spring packed with crime.'

'I appreciate that, Mister Giotto,' she said, leaning back. 'I am prepared to pay a substantial wage.'

'It's pretty substantial whether you're prepared to pay it or not,' Henry said.

'Fine, then, Mister Giotto,' said Lady Constance. 'We are agreed. You will recover my dog for me?'

'I shall apply my acumen to the problem.'

'You know,' said Lady Constance, a few tears running down a well-powdered cheek, 'I'm relieved. I feared you would refuse.'

'I'm eccentric, I know,' said the great detective, 'but not to the point of refusing money.'

'Here is my card,' said Lady Constance. 'My house is at your disposal. I shall be there myself at all times.'

'Ring me if there's any further news, Lady Constance,' said Henry, getting up to escort her out.

'Good-bye, Mister Giotto,' she said. 'Good-bye, Mister Duck.'

'Cheerio,' I said.

When we had the office to ourselves again, Henry said: 'Hmmm.'

He paced up and down the worn carpet. He looked out the window for a moment, and swung around with his hands clasped at his back.

'Yes, yes, yes,' he said. 'Come on, Duck, we're going out.'

'Please call me Belemus,' I said.

'Right. And you call me Henry,' he said. 'But hurry on.'

We went out of the offices and down a rickety stairway. We passed out into a bright hilly street.

'Up to the tube station,' said Henry. 'We won't take the car, I think.'

We walked up past a Woolworth's shop and a flower-shop. Henry bought our tickets, and we went down in a lift into the ground. We waited on the platform with a crowd of silent strangers. There was a distant rushing noise, like a wave by the sea, and a square of yellow lights plucked into view inside the tunnel. I thought it was the front of the train, but it was only a panel of bulbs on the breast of the engine. The train was much bigger than that, so it was out of the tunnel and into the glare of the station lights before you expected it to be. We stepped in.

'It's funny, you know,' said Henry, 'How one thing follows another.'

Having said this he lapsed into a silence for the length of the journey.

We came up into the sun again. There was a street with a number of restaurants with Chinese signs.

'There's a man we must talk to,' said Henry. 'Don't, when we find him, put your hand in your pocket. He'll knife you before you get half-way in. Got gun-fever. Thinks they're everywhere.'

'Okay,' I said.

We walked along the warm pavement.

'Where's this?' I said, hurrying beside his tweed elbow.

'Don't you know?' he said. 'It's Soho.'

'Oh,' I said.

'Here we are,' he said, pausing at a gaping door. 'Up we go, Belemus.'

We climbed for a while up stairs even more rickety than Henry's, till we reached the very top. There was an attic door, with the thin lines of knife-marks on it, and a black circle painted roughly on the wood.

'Dear, *dear*,' said Henry, 'I hope he's still with us.'

He knocked on the door.

'Hoose thir?' said a voice.

'Henry Green,' said Henry Giotto. 'Got a few questions for you, Jock.'

'Don't want noo questions, laddie. Lave me aloon.'

'There's a fiver in it, Jock,' said Henry through the keyhole. A man's got to eat.'

'Aye, *thaat's* true enow,' said the voice. We heard footsteps cross the floor. Chains and locks were freed. The thick door opened an inch.

'Ah suppose thaat is Muster Green, and no some rowten thuggie?'

'Of course,' said Henry. 'It's I and my colleague, young Mister Duck. We're out on an investigation.'

'Okae,' said Jock. 'Cum in then.'

We entered the attic. A few old cases were at angles on the floor. All over the walls there were books, leather-bound books and large books like atlases.

'How's the collection, Jock?' said Henry.

'Och, you niver know, Muster Green,' said Jock with a laugh. 'It's a shiftin' markih, an' noo mustake.'

'Good, good,' said Henry.

'Ye'll sit doon, will ye no?' said Jock.

'Best to stand, Jock,' said Henry. 'You lead an active life in here. Never know when some angry hood's going to burst in on top of us.'

'Aye,' said Jock, laughing. 'Thaat's the truth.'

'Mister Duck here and I have been engaged to recover a valuable dog. Has there been any talk?'

'Aboot dawgs? Nay, no that I knoo of.'

'Are you certain?' said Henry, leaning closer. 'The theft happened last night, in the early evening, I believe.'

'Noo, noo, thir hasna been a whusper. And I wus oot tidee, heard a lotta taulk.'

'Fine, Jock, fine, that's very interesting.'

Henry handed Jock a five-pound note, and the Scotsman pocketed it with a smile.

'Any time, Muster Green. Ye knoo Jock's yer mon.'

Down in the street Henry said:

'Well, Belemus, we mustn't be down-hearted. Sometimes no news tells you as much as an hour's information. If Jock has heard nothing there has been nothing to hear.'

We went back to Hampstead, and Henry stopped beside a ramshackle bubble-car. It was his.

'We'll look at this woman's address, Belemus, and see where she lives. I think we must pay her a visit.'

The little card she had given him said:

Lady Constance Heather-Heather
Pook House
Pook
Pookshire

'Righto,' said Henry. 'I'll skip up to the office and we'll be off. I hear the tinkle of my phone.'

When he came back he said:

'That was Lady Constance. She has received a note from the thief, or thieves. It says simply: "Burn your house down or you will never see your dog again". This I regard as fascinating,' said Henry.

We got into his car and headed off through the afternoon traffic. A few hours later we passed a sign that said:

Welcome to Pookshire

After that, about ten miles on, we arrived at the village of Pook. We asked a local where the manor was.

'Pook House, you mean, sirs? Them big gates further on. The big black gates, sir.'

'Thank you,' said Henry. 'By the way, how long has her Ladyship been living in Pook?'

'Pook, sir? Hundreds of years, sir. Her family, that is, sir, the Heathers of Pook, you see, sir.'

'Ah,' said Henry. 'No connection with Blackpool, then?'

'Blackpool, sir? I don't know how's you mean, sir.'

'Righto,' said Henry. 'Thanks.'

The little car drove on, leaving the local examining the shilling Henry had tossed him.

Henry made his usual comment:

'Hmmm.'

We turned in through the black gates, and chugged up

a wooded drive. It was about a mile long.

'Must be a *very* big borzoi,' said Henry.

We parked in front of a smallish manor-house.

'A rich but conservative taste,'said Henry, looking the façade over.

A man in a black uniform answered the door to us.

'Henry Giotto,' said Henry. 'I'm expected, I think.'

'Of course, sir,' said the man. 'I'm Thomas. Please, come this way.'

Thomas the chauffeur-butler showed us into a drawing-room on the other side of the hall. Lady Constance was seated there in a large chair.

'There you are, Mister Giotto,' she said in her high voice.

She gave us tea and cakes, and after ten minutes the telephone rang.

Lady Constance looked at us both, and picked up the receiver.

'Yes?' she said. 'Tonight? But surely...'

She rattled the phone, but it was no use.

'That was the thieves,' she said. 'They insist I set fire to the old place tonight. Mister Giotto, Mister Duck, what shall I do?'

'We're not sure yet, Lady Constance,' said Henry. 'We must take this as it comes. I suppose the dog is essential to your well-being and all that?'

'Mister Giotto, you're not suggesting I let her be...'

'Just a thought, just a thought. Now, if I may look over the house a bit, just the place where the dog usually sleeps and so on.'

'She's always loose about the place. Of course, just the downstairs part of the house,' she added quickly. 'You can look about there if you want.'

'Righto,' said Henry. 'You stay and talk to her Ladyship, Belemus. I won't be long. Can I speak to Thomas? Where will I find him?'

'Give him a minute to get back,' said Lady Constance.

'He's gone for some shopping.'

'Fine,' said Henry, giving his hands a loud smack. 'Won't be long.'

Henry went out. Lady Constance slumped in her chair, her considerable shoulders hunching.

'My nerves are gone,' she said. 'Gone. Shot through.'

'It must be upsetting,' I said. 'Losing your dog, I mean. Your house in danger.'

'How can I burn it?' she said. 'I'd rather burn myself.'

'Don't say that,' I said. 'Henry will find your dog before that will be necessary.'

Henry come back some time later.

'I've talked to Thomas,' he said. 'He knows nothing. Of course, he was with you when it happened. Or I suppose he was. He couldn't have slipped back while you were at the Jackson-Walpoles?'

'No, no, we, I mean they, live a good fifty miles away.'

'I see, yes, yes,' said Henry, sitting down. 'Well, if you'll leave my colleague and myself alone for a bit, Lady Constance. We must discuss this case freely, you understand.'

'Of course,' said her Ladyship. 'Excuse me, I didn't think.'

She clumped across the rich carpets and left us to ourselves.

'That Thomas fellow,' said Henry, 'most nervous disposition. Can't make him out. Not the criminal type at all. Perhaps he's jumpy by nature.'

'Did he say anything suspicious?'

'No,' said Henry. 'Just a replica of what Lady Constance told us. Pit-a-pat, actually. Still, there might be nothing in that.'

I noticed a new white wire running along the wainscoting, and I pointed it out to Henry.

What he said was:

'Hmmm.'

In the late afternoon Lady Constance served us a light dinner, in case the night ahead was too full of events to eat. We returned to the drawing-room.

'By the way, Lady Constance,' Henry said, 'have you had any electrical work done in the house lately?'

'No, I don't think so,' she said.

'Ah,' said Henry.

A minute later the phone rang. Lady Constance looked as agitated as before, and picked it up.

'Is that you?' she said. 'One hour's time? Oh I don't think I can!' she cried, her voice breaking deeper with emotion. We heard the dead whirr of the phone.

She cleared her throat and said:

'It must be done within the hour, or they will put Dolly down. I can't bear that to happen, Mister Giotto. I'm going to have to fire the old house.'

'Calm down, Lady Constance. It might not come to that. Why on earth do they want the house burned down? That puzzles me. Where is Thomas? I want to talk to him again.'

'Thomas is out shopping,' said Lady Constance.

'At six o'clock?' said Henry. 'Again?'

'He likes shopping,' she said.

'Where is the garage?' asked Henry. 'I'll wait for him there.'

'Mister Giotto,' said her Ladyship, rising. 'I don't see what good it'll do talking to Thomas. He knows absolutely nothing about anything. He's just a chauffeur and a butler. In fact if anything he's rather a nuisance from time to time. I'm going now to lay paraffin about the house in case the worst comes to the worst. I must save Dolly's life.

'Of course,' said Henry, jumping up. 'That is not in question. We shall save the dog no matter what. Lay your paraffin if you like. But don't do anything more till you have word from me.'

'If you say so,' she said, and left the room.

100

'Belemus,' said Henry, 'I think we'll follow this wire of yours. I have noticed it starts from the telephone. Quite a neat job, as you can judge for yourself. Where it leads to remains to be seen.'

We walked around the edge of the room following the white wire. It slipped out beneath the door and ran across the hall under the carpet. At the hall-door it reappeared, and travelled down the side of the broad steps. It trailed across the gravel sweep, and onto the lawn, concealed beneath stones and grass.

At each twist of its direction, Henry murmured:
'Hmmm.'

It went on over the lawn, and disappeared into a wood. We were about three minutes from the house, and for a second we heard the barking of a dog.

'Belemus,' said Henry. 'We're getting warm. Though who is heating the water is another question.'

We tracked the wire among the trees. In a clearing it snaked to a rustic hut and ran in the open window. Henry and I crept up to the door. It was beginning to get dark. We put our ears to the panels of bark.

We heard the familiar sound of someone dialling on a telephone. Just four numbers. We caught the lilt of a voice saying:

'I'm ringing for the last time, sir.'

'That voice,' whispered Henry, 'belongs to Thomas the chauffeur-butler, or I'm not the son of Jeremiah Giotto.'

'You can go ahead now, sir,' said Thomas's quiet voice.

Henry gave the door a heave with his shoulder, and we burst into the murky hut.

'What do you mean, Thomas?' Henry cried. 'To whom are you talking?'

A tall stately dog jumped to its feet and began to bark at us in a miserable fashion. Thomas told it to be quiet and it obeyed.

'Mister Giotto!' said Thomas. 'Mister Duck! I'm fair ruined now!'

101

'What are you talking about, man?' said Henry. 'Out with it, quickly!'

'They'll hang me now for sure,' said Thomas, and burst into tears. The borzoi came over and licked his ear.

'Oh dash it,' said Henry. 'Just tell me what's up. I'll help you. You're not the kidnapping type, Thomas, I knew that from the start.'

'No, sir,' said Thomas, looking up into our faces. 'Not the kidnapping type truly, sir. The murderin' type.'

'Nonsense. What do you mean?'

'It was like this, Mister Giotto. When Sir Timothy Feather-Feather died, her Ladyship went into deep mourning. I thought she'd never get over it. She was so brave about it too, and it was three years before her spirit quietened, and she was calm. It was a lovely thing to see, sir, a lovely thing. I was glad for her. She bought herself this dog here, Dolorus, which means sorrow you see, sir, and she and I lived on gently from day to day. She didn't lack for anything, I waited on her faithfully. Then one day Mister Jackson-Walpole came over from the neighbouring estate, 'bout fifty miles from here. He was an old friend of the late Sir Timothy's, they knew each other in Africa, sir. Well her Ladyship changed, sir. Mister Walpole's a big clumsy man, sir, he's no beauty I can tell you, but he's a straight sort, and he was kind to her. She fell in love with him, sir, and well, it near broke my heart. I'm only an old servant, I know, sir, but love's love, sir, love's love.

'They were standing at the head of the stairs one night, sir, and Mister Walpole was just setting off for home. I heard him from the shadows propose marriage, and I heard her accept. I couldn't stand it, sir. I rushed out to stop them, plead with them, tell her how I felt, sir, when I trips on that old bit of carpet I should have removed years ago. I went banging into her sweet Ladyship, and she plummeted like a little sack, sir, to the hall below. Dead, sir, quite dead. Mister Jackson-Walpole caught me before

102

I went toppling after her, I was that off-balance. Now Mister Walpole's a gentleman, sir. He believes in looking after the servants. Africa, you know, sir. He never mentioned a thing about the whole messy business, he just puts her Ladyship in a bedroom above in the house, and makes up this dog-stealing plan. He's going to burn the house, sir, and slip away home in the darkness. He's hoping you'll find her Ladyship's body in the burned-out house, sir, hard to identify, you know, and think she decided to go down with the old place, that sort of thing. Very natural, you know, among the ancient gentry.'

'Very natural, my foot!' said Henry. 'What a pair of fools you both are. The death was an accident!'

'That may well be, sir, but at this moment Mister Jackson-Walpole's setting fire to the house. I just talked to him on this phone I rigged up. He doesn't know I've been deviated, sir.'

'But who's the big woman posing as her Ladyship?' said Henry. 'Where does she come in?'

'That's Mister Walpole, sir, in woman's clothing.'

I remembered the strange masculine way the woman had sitting in Henry's office, and the high voice breaking on the telephone.

'You have it all now,' said Thomas.

Henry rushed out of the hut.

When Thomas and I and the borzoi reached the open ground around the house, I half-expected to see the sky full of red flames, and hear in the distance the clanging of a fire-engine. But Henry and Mister Jackson-Walpole, still in his striped dress, were standing on the gravel in front of an intact manor.

'Stopped him just in time,' Henry called to me. 'Had the match lit in his hand, all ready.'

Mister Walpole was standing more like a man now. In a deep booming voice he said:

'Dashed bad luck. Pity you're such a clever bounder, Giotto, or the plan would've worked splendidly.'

'Well,' said Henry. 'I don't know about that. The thing now is to explain the whole thing slowly and thoroughly to the police.'

How sensible Henry Giotto was, I thought. The next moment I was lying in my bed.

X THE SETTING SUN

AS I plodded to school the following morning the sun turned traditional and came out. It crept into Merrion Square. I could see through a tangle of bushes a flow of grass, and wooded mounds, private in the locked square.

I passed the traffic-lights and was walking in a desert. It wasn't a bad desert. There were no sand-dunes or mirages. The ground was stony, with some stunted trees. Off to the left and right were mountains with flat tops.

My hair grew hot – the sun was like a hand on the crown of my head.

I thought I noticed horses in a field of rocks in the distance. The next moment there was nothing.

Among the boulders I heard no clatter of hooves. In the silence I saw a flash of skin. I kept going – there was nothing else I could do.

Four Indians flattened me on the ground. They laughed and got off me. I decided to walk on, but they blocked the way. One loped off and fetched their horses. They mounted, leaving me standing among them. They made a whoop. An arm reached down and swept me up. The horses swung away.

I joggled. If I twisted too far one way or the other the Indian clutched me back on balance.

I could view only the rocky earth, and the sky and the mountain sweeping crazily around.

At their village they flung me into the dust. A band of children hurried over and cast dry dung at me.

There were more braves in the camp, and older men. Women stepped out from the conical tents.

It was late afternoon, judging by the slant of the sun. It was going down in a blaze of red, and the Indians stood looking at it. It disappeared behind the mountain, slipping along the sharp ridge.

The Indians who had captured me came over. They took a limb each and pulled me into the air.

I was dragged to a stake in the centre of the camp and bound up against it.

A half-light was in the camp, a yellow afterglow of the sun. Fires were lit among the wigwams, and there was a to-ing and fro-ing of the women. The smoke went up into the evening. The men lay talking. The children were caught and carried to bed.

The village had dinner. They ate fried meat or fish, which had been lying in layers on the sides of the tents.

They seemed a colour-loving tribe. Their wigwams were reds and blues, and I could glimpse inside blankets and tapestries.

After dinner there was dancing and wavering songs.

A breeze came up the hill, some wind with a tooth of ice.

They settled for the night. There was no-one around soon except one Indian at the edge of the camp. I tried to loosen my ropes, working at my wrists. It was useless.

Wolves cried across the plains through the night. The watchman nodded off. A moon walked over the sky, like a lantern in a giant's hand. There was the endless thin note of an insect somewhere.

Before the sun rose again the camp awoke. The place was all noise and laughter, with the clank of earthern pots and the splash of water. Braves stepped out from the tents and stretched in the gloom. They called out greetings to one another.

A squaw came with a bundle of brushwood and spread it about my feet. She went back and forward to the woodpile, with her hips swinging. After a few journeys the wood was to my knees.

The braves hoofed their pintos down the hill. The women chatted and screamed at their children. Dogs tried to steal things and had stones thrown at them. I had a hunger like an enemy. I felt it more in my chest than in my stomach. My tongue was as dry as a stone.

In the afternoon the men returned in a flurry of dust, with nothing to show for the day's hunting. They pushed their way around the camp. The children crept off into the outskirts of the village.

Towards evening the cooking started. The white-haired elders appeared and grouped themselves in front of me. They left a good ten feet between us.

Women laid out bowls of food, and the braves took their places. The children hovered at the rim, watching and eating with interested eyes.

I imagined I spotted a scrap of blue above the village. But the Indians noticed nothing.

There was drink passed among the braves. They got rowdy. Drums beat like horses streaming for ever across a plain.

A dance began. They flung their arms about, following each other around the pole. They danced hour after hour, till the children were asleep on the ground.

The chant of the braves and the storm of the drums increased. The night sparked. I could see faces lit up as the torch moved here and there – old and young faces, brown and creased, happy, alert.

A brave threw the lit brand suddenly in amid the wood. Twigs caught, wrapping the stouter wood in little flames. I saw children with their hands to their cheeks. The dancers shook and wailed.

A figure burst into their midst. It was a big muddy beast with white feathers. There was a toss of white hair on its head, and a pair of bright eyes. The animal was making a rumpus like a steam-engine: whoo! whoo!

The braves fled into the darkness. The children vanished like monkeys. The elders put their heads in their hands and didn't look.

The animal crowded near me. It cut my knots, snatched me, and hurried off roaring up the mountainside. Its skin was slimy where it touched me. I caught a last sight of the camp behind me. The fire swept in hot pillars up the pole.

'Now, young feller,' said the creature, cloaked in shadow, 'we gotta skip outa here quick as rabbits. Else we're scalped for sure.'

We reached a water-hole with a horse and mule tacked-up and ready. The creature plunged into the pool and dashed its arms about. It stepped out. It was a tall wet man. He had blue jeans on and a shirt. His hair was straggling down his cheeks. Here and there the mud he had been covered in still stuck to him.

'That wus my best feather-pillow I jus used on yor account, nipper, I hope you 'preciate it.'

'Gosh, I do,' I said.

'Hop you up on that mule there, boy, and let's be away before the injuns catch thar breath on us. I bin watchin' you that at the stake from these hills all day, a-lookin' for the main chance. Hate to put all that waitin' to waste.'

He climbed dripping into his saddle. I did the same. The mule was hitched to the horse. I had only to hang on.

We went up the rugged side of the mountain and crossed the flat top and descended. The mule broke into a bouncy gallop to match the horse's canter, and we hurried down into the plain.

The animals travelled for the rest of the night. The man didn't look round to speak.

By dawn we came to fertile land, and we trotted among expanses of grass. We turned at a river and rode through the shallow water at the edge for an hour.

107

'Yer a good young un,' the man said as he lifted me down. 'There's not many youngsters could hold up like that. You cin rest for a space now, an' fuel up.'

He laid me on the grass and gave me water and food.

'Ain't carryin' no fancy vittals,' he said, 'but yer sure welcome to the bit I have.'

I fell off into a sleep. I woke when the sun was higher in the sky. I saw the man standing by the river, his hands in his pockets, watching the water flow by him. He had wide shoulders, and his legs were long and bandy. The side of his face was weathered and old. About sixty maybe. He had a large gray hat. His locks hung down from under the battered brim. He caught a sound of my moving behind him, and turned.

'You an' I best be shiftin',' he said. 'Them injuns might reckon on a double roastin' party.'

I felt better. I liked the sight of the streaming river and the miles and miles of grasses.

'Sure is a fine little country, eh, boy?' the man said. 'Now what the hell you wanderin' around in it fur? Have to wait a few more years tillin you cin come out here on yer lonesome I reckon.'

'I got stuck out here,' I said. 'My name's Belemus.'

'Sure, Bel, how do. Ma name's ordinarily Ned. Some calls me Mister Bailey. But the injuns call me White Fire, which I likes bettern them others.'

'White fire,' I said.

'Sure, boy. But you calls me Ned. Ned's okay by me too.'

We saddled up the horse and mule and continued along the river.

'We gotta cross this feller here,' said Ned, 'iffin we want to git to Tombstone. Where was you headed to begin with?'

'I'm not completely sure,' I said.

'Wal Tombstone'll do as good as that,' he said.

'Where were you going to yourself, Ned?'

108

'Hell, I wus like you. I ain't headed nowheres. I wus up the North Country all winter trappin' beaver, and now I'm jus driftin' aroun'. I got me a few dollars'll last me till the fall. Then I reckon I'll think me some more. Jus about like that, you know. Mebbe I'll do me some army work. I don't know.'

He pulled up his horse. There was a jut of land sticking out in the water.

'Reckon this'll be the best place, nipper,' he said. 'Jus brace up them leg muscles of yourn. Don't you go fallin' off that ol' mule. River's worse than injuns. Jes hang on, Bel.'

He plunged his horse in, and the current took him and he was moving down-river. I hesitated.

'Come on thar, Bel,' Ned Bailey shouted. 'Plunge that critter in!'

I kicked the mule forward. He fell like a boulder into the water and I thought he wasn't going to float. I gripped hard and the mule swam like crazy. He swam like a paddle-steamer. Ned reached the shore. A minute later my old mule got here, and next second we were panting on dry land. Ned gave a shout, and slapped my back.

'You sure is the most ornery juvinile I ever did meet!' he said. 'Hell you crossed that river like a crocodeel.'

'Your mule is wonderful,' I said. 'He's as stout as a buffalo.'

'Sure is!' said Ned. 'Didn't give no fifty dollars for a jack-rabbit, boy!'

Ned led the way. He sang. His horse ambled in the grassy heat:

> 'I am a lonesome feller
> I hunt the mountain trail
> when a feller calls me yeller
> I shoots him in the tail.'

'That's a good song,' he said. 'Little ol' shoemaker in

109

Wyoming made that song, Bel!'

I laughed.

'You know, Bel, I'm a-ridin' and a-travellin' round and I never see nothing as pretty as nature. Towns ain't fur me, boy, this ol' wide back-country's fur me. And sure enough peoples is buyin' it up, stockin' her up with cattle, fencin' the wild country further and further. Hell, Bel, come five years thar'll be a road 'long here, and we'll be passin' farmers' wagons and mail-riders and merchants and army-riders and all sorts of strange critters you never seen 'long here afore. Reckon the old West has seen its days, Bel, reckon it has. Beaver nearly run out up North too, bad winter.'

'Ned, don't you get lonely out here on your own?' I said.

'Never, Bel. Had me a wife once in Colorada, Indian woman, good gal. Died some twenty years 'go. Damn pity. Had me a sad ol' time that time, Bel. Drinkin' and a-goin' to the bad. One days I just up and head out inta the wilderness, kind of crazy like, thinkin' I'd put an ol' bullit wheren it ort not ta be, and say my last farewell. Hell I was so happy jes to be out here in the big nowhere I started a-singin'. Then I started a-lookin' around, and hell I felt like I wus come home.'

We camped that night in a gulley of rocks. Ned kept our fire small. He was worried about the Indians, but he didn't think they'd follow that far. He wrapped me in a blanket.

I woke in a thin light, the sky spread above me. Ned was making coffee in a billy can, and had breakfast heating on a pan.

'Hell I wish we had us a dog, Bel. Dogs is a helluva critter in the mornin'. Leapin' and a-playin'. Yes sir, wish we had us a dog.'

In the afternoon we came to the first of the fences, wooden stakes mile after mile in the wild grass. We passed a herd of longhorn cattle, and cowboys keeping a

110

watch over them.

'Hi there, Mister Bailey!' the men called, and Ned gave a slow wave of his arm.

'Sure is a fine ol' day!' he called back.

We reached the edge of a town. The sun was going down in front of us, and there was a glare over the roof-tops that made it hard to see.

'Tombstone,' said Ned. 'Thit wild ol' girl.'

We were going to ride on in when a voice from the glare said:

'Git down offa that critter, Ned Bailey.'

We came to a halt. Ned peered into the light of the setting sun. We could see the shape of a man, standing in the middle of the road. There were other shapes scuttering along the sidewalks with a clunk clunk, and the sound of doors being closed.

'Now jes who might that be?' said Ned. 'I know you, boy?'

'Nope,' said the outline. 'But I knows you. You're Ned Bailey, and I aim to kill you dayed.'

'You buildin' a repitation, boy?' said Ned.

'I sure is,' said the other man. 'An' yor jus 'bout the last feller can help do it. Don't make 'em now'days like they made *you*, Ned Bailey.'

Just then a motor car came hooting along out of the town. It was old-fashioned, hardly more than a carriage without a horse.

'Damn,' said Ned. 'What in hell is that?'

'That's a car,' I said. 'An automobile.'

'The world's gettin' too ornery for me, Bel,' said Ned. 'Hell, what a useless contraption!'

'Listen here, Bailey!' the man said. 'You don't take no heed of that thing! You look to me now!'

'Well, boy,' said Ned. 'Seein' as the future don't look like to be a payin' business, I'd as soon fight you as not. But I'm a sure good man with a shootin'-iron, boy, and like as not I'll put you in your coffin.'

111

'I'll take the risk, Ned Bailey!' said the man, and I could hear a tremor in his voice.

'I'm gettin' off ma horse, mister,' said Ned.

He climbed down. He was stiff after the ducking he'd had. He gave his horse a pat, and he gave the mule a hard look. He strode out into the centre of the road, and faced the sun.

'So long, Bel. Nice knowin' ye.'

I saw the outline of the other man move. There was a blaze of fire from his guns. Ned had got his gun out first. I had heard it give a solid click, and no more. His tall figure stood for a second, and buckled.

'Hell,' said the other man. 'I got him. I got Ned Bailey.'

Ned dropped to the dust. I climbed off the mule. I went over to Ned.

'Sure is a funny thing,' he whispered to me, his face half pressed in the dirt. 'Sure is an awful funny thing.'

There was a red wound over his heart. The man who had shot him came up and looked at Ned's gun.

'Darn,' he said, spinning the barrels.

'So long, boys,' said Ned to us with his last breath.

'Darn,' said the man, showing me the gun. 'What in hell've I dun? The ol' critter didn't have no bullets left.'

I looked at the man with one long look, and I looked at Ned's face on the edge of Tombstone. I heard another motor car coming up behind us, and turned to face it. It was the 7A bus.

"I got him. I got Ned Bailey"

XI UNDER THE CLOTH

O UTSIDE the kitchen door I tried to make myself look
awake. I walked in with a smile.

'You look tired, Belemus,' said my father.

Oh well.

I slumped at the table and yawned. I had spent an hour
in secret the night before watching the sky above my
window.

I reached for the salt-cellar and found it changed into a
capsule. It had Bacon and Eggs printed on it.

I was in a low room, with a machine. I tried the
capsule. A flood of flavour released in my mouth.

The machine had a lot of buttons. I pressed HOT
CHOCOLATE. That was a pill as well. A warm stream
trickled down my throat.

I stepped to the door. It slid, and showed a corridor.

The chrome-yellow passage stopped in a blank wall at
each end. The door next to mine said SICK-BAY.

Down the corridor I came to the largest entrance. The
leaves opened. I entered a high room, with one whole wall
a window. Beyond the window I saw stars and planets in
a black void.

I sat in a chair at the back of the room. I was wearing a
white overall. Stitched across my right breast was the
word Captain.

A control panel was in front of the chair. I pushed a
button tagged COMPUTER and a machine whirred. I
activated DATA FOR MISSION.

A screen flashed:

Ship: Albatross 14
Captain: Belemus Duck
Mission: Investigation and Rescue of Cormorant 3
Reason: Disappearance of Cormorant 3

Last Location
of Lost Craft: The Elder Galaxy
Nearest Planet: Landia

I switched off the buttons. I pushed in DESTINATION.
The screen told me:

Elder Galaxy
Planet Landia

I leaned back. The door slid behind me, and I swung
round. A pillar of metal on wheels came in. The metal
was polished, and towards the top was a section like a
loud-speaker.

'Hello,' I said. Do you know who I am?'

The robot spoke with a strangled gargle, but his words
were clear enough:

'Affirmative. Captain Belemus Duck, commander of
the Albatross.'

'I suppose that's true for the moment. And you are?'

'Robot Fing. Abbreviation for Finger. Number X 16.'

'Are there any others on the ship?' I said. 'Humans or
robots?'

'Negative. Not necessary. Two suffices.'

'Fine,' I said. 'What do we do now?'

'Long journey ahead. Should be in deep freeze.
Question: Why are you not?'

'I'm not sure. But if I should be let's see to it right
away.'

'Affirmative. Follow.'

Fing hummed round again, and trundled out of the
control room. He led me down the corridor to the sick-
bay.

'I'm not ill, Fing,' I said.

'Deep freeze kept here. Follow.'

There was a glass bed in the centre of the floor, with a
transparent case hanging above it from the ceiling.

There were many machines, one called TIME REVERSAL MACHINE, and another BONE REPLACEMENT CENTRE, and another INTRICATE BRAIN-SURGERY COMPLEX.

'This is well equipped,' I said. 'Is there a doctor?'

'Negative. Automatic. Lie on freezer unit.'

I climbed on the bed. Fing flicked a switch with an arm he brought out of his body. The glass cover above me descended. I felt a touch of icy vapour seeping into the enclosed space.

When I woke, Fing was at the switch, as if he had merely shut and opened the freezer unit.

'You are hungry,' his crackling voice said. 'Three years in deep freeze.'

'What?' I said, looking down to see if I had aged. I was the same as before.

'Repeat? Question: Is my voice defective?'

'No, that's all right. I was only surprised. What is our position?'

'Five hours two minutes seven seconds from outer atmosphere of planet Landia.'

We went back to the control room.

'What sort of planet is it?' I said.

'Atmosphere considered as Earth. Otherwise data unknown. Planet previously unexplored. Difficulty.'

'What difficulty?' I said.

'Unknown.'

'Has anyone been here before?'

'Affirmative. Year 2081, two missions – result: unknown. 2088, one mission – result: unknown. 2098, one mission, Cormorant 3 – result: under investigation.'

'By us, you mean?'

'Affirmative.'

'I see. One of a long line, unfortunately.'

'Affirmative.'

'Do we have a better chance than the others?' I said.

'Affirmative. Advanced. Cormorant 3 last ship of old

116

type. Advanced outer protection. Atomic Force Shield replaced by Bi-nuclear Wall.'

'Oh,' I said.

'Further questions?'

'No, that's all I can think of,' I said.

Fing turned to go.

'Where are you off to, Fing?' I asked.

'Engines must be checked.'

'How long will that take?'

'Three hours. Seven miles of tunnel to traverse.'

'Gosh,' I said. 'It must be a large ship.'

'Affirmative.'

And he went.

I sat back. We were passing through an empty part of space. I presumed the ship had reached the Elder Galaxy. I checked, and the computer confirmed it. We had been within the galaxy for six months.

Far ahead beyond the window I sighted a dot of blue, with a centre of white. I pressed LIGHT SCREEN, and a plastic curtain moved down the window.

I looked at the planet closely. It was on its own in an infinity of space. After an hour it was the size of a football. A mass of blue was whirling about it, except for a space in the middle that was the dazzling light. It was like a sea creature, luring the ship towards its mouth.

Something struck the outside of the Albatross. I rocked forward and knocked against the panel. Information dashed onto the screen, and for a minute I was busy restoring things. I strapped myself into the seat. Again the craft was hit, and I searched the panel for the right button. At last I found it: BI-NUCLEAR WALL.

The next blow was muffled. I asked the computer what had struck us: Unknown.

That worried me. I asked it whether it had been weaponry of some kind: Negative.

Whatever it was, it was still bombarding the protecting wall. I strained to see anything outside that could be causing it. There was nothing there. Or did I see a series of lights, flashing as they swept towards us from the planet? I asked the computer for further information. This time it had something worked out:

Atmospheric Storm
Description: Previously Unencountered

I wondered if the other ships had run into this and had been unable to defend themselves.

The blue clouds were more distinct. They were flowing in seas around the planet's outer atmosphere. The section of light had lost its glare, so I raised the screen.

There seemed to be shadow and brightness on the planet's surface, or it might have been oceans and mountains. I asked the computer why the centre was no longer blinding: Unknown.

An hour later Landia was an orb in front of me. The hole in the cloud was big. The battering of the storm stopped, and Fing returned from the engines.

'Any damage to the ship?' I said.

'One mile of engine torn away.'

'Is that bad?'

'Negative. Affirmative.'

'You mean yes and no? Well, will we be able to return to Earth?'

'Affirmative.'

'That's all right then, isn't it?'

'Negative. Auxiliary freezer unit removed from operation. Survivor from Cormorant 3, if still breathing, cannot be carried home.'

'I see. That complicates things.'

'Affirmative.'

'Do we have an entry flight worked out?'

'Negative.'

'Do we do that now?'

'Affirmative.'

Fing made some calculations at the flight entry section of the computer. He pulled a tape from a slot and plugged it in.

'Analysis of cloud,' he said. 'Detrimental poison. Corrosive. Deadly to metal. Bi-nuclear Wall insufficient. Must enter by the gap.'

'Okay,' I said. 'I agree. Do we know yet if the planet's inner atmosphere is breathable?'

'Affirmative,' said Fing, working at the computer. 'Reasonable air. Slightly heavy in oxygen. Breathable.'

'Good,' I said. 'I hope the corrosive cloud has no contact with the surface, for your sake.'

'Negative. No contact.'

'Then we must make ready to land. We're nearly at the gap now.'

'Affirmative.'

Fing slid over and stood at my side. We watched the front of the ship draw closer to the gap. The computer kept us clear of the outer rims of the blue cloud, though it reported a strong magnetic pull.

We were in. The under-side of the cloud was a silver colour, which reflected light onto the planet's surface.

'Perpetual day,' said Fing.

We were looking at a curve of water. Fing put the spaceship into a break. We entered the inner atmosphere, and the auxiliary engines burst into life. Our ship orbited, so we could map out the place. We were flying in an atmosphere like Earth's, and the silence of space was gone. The roar of our engines was a surprise.

'Can't we help that noise?' I said. 'I can't think.'

'Affirmative,' said Fing. 'Press QUIET.'

The relief was immediate.

'Phew,' I said.

'Affirmative,' said Fing.

'This is an odd place,' I said. 'The water goes on for ever. Can we have a computer analysis?'

Fing worked it out swiftly. The screen said:

Nature of Sea: Fresh water
Extent: Entire planet

'Gosh,' I said. 'It does go on for ever. Is there no land at all?'

The computer told us: Polar Islands.

'Polar?' I said. 'Does that mean they're frozen?'

'Negative,' said Fing. 'Climate here is all the same. Sub-tropical equivalent.'

'Let's head then for the North Pole,' I said. 'And we'll have a look.'

Fing swung the ship in an arc, and we rocketed to the North. The sea beneath us was as calm as a lake. There was no sign of life.

'Land ahead,' said Fing.

We saw a circular island. There was something like grass growing on it. It was blue. The computer said:

Primitive Vegetation
No Humanoids
No Animal or Insect Life

'This is odd, Fing,' I said. 'If there are grasses you'd expect other forms of life. It's hard to imagine that only this blue stuff has evolved and nothing else. It doesn't make much sense.'

'Affirmative. Earth logic absent from Landia.'

'There's no trace of a spaceship down there,' I said, when we had crossed the length and breadth of the island. 'We'd better go South.'

The ship arced again, and we travelled above the still sea.

The computer came to life:

Remains of Spacecraft on Sea-bed
No Survivor
Jackdaw 22

Year: 2081
Cause of Crash: Destruction by Battering.

'What mission is that? The first one?'

'Affirmative.'

'Then we must assume the others are lost on the sea-bed too?' I said.

'Affirmative. Negative.'

'Alright,' I said, 'I see what you mean. We must examine the South Polar island first.'

We reached it a while afterwards. It was a larger landmass than the North pole, and we decided to fly around the edge.

'Look Fing,' I said. 'A spaceship.'

There was a craft floating in the water, with cables mooring it to the land.

'Which of the ships could float?' I said.

'All.'

'That must be the lucky one. Take us down, Fing.'

'Seven miles of spaceship?' Fing said.

'Oh. Is that not the procedure?'

'Negative, Captain. Hover Albatross. We take the Link Ship.'

'Of course. Come on then.'

We hurried along the corridor to the lift. We whistled down to a flight-deck, where a shuttle-craft was parked. I clambered in. Fing entered by a hatch, and joined me in the front.

A metal wall hauled up, and we jetted the Link Ship out. We were breathing the atmosphere, or I was, and apart from a thick taste about it, it felt alright.

We roared down from the Albatross. I looked back at it. It was an enormous craft, with miles of engines dwarfing the control section. I noticed a piece that had broken off, and a sea of wires and smashed machinery across the wound.

We landed near the docked spaceship. There was the

same blue grass on this island, a soft stuff growing out of hard rock. I walked with Fing to the ship. I made out in battered letters on the nose: Cormorant 3.

'So that last mission made it this far,' I said. 'Who was on board?'

'Captain Alfred Digsby. And one robot, W 2.'

The Cormorant was a biggish ship, but it hadn't the scale of the Albatross. Everywhere there were holes and bits missing – marks of the 'invisible' storm. A stairway led down from the control section, and Fing and I rattled up.

At the top we reached a corridor. We looked in the sick-bay. There were none of the sophisticated machines there, and the freezer module looked more risky.

We were on the point of leaving when Fing motored to a metal cabinet. He turned a dial, and the metal opened. Inside was a robot like Fing, with one of its plates open, and wires sticking out. Screwdrivers and drills were scattered around it. Someone had tried to mend it and failed.

'Beyond repair?' I asked.

'Affirmative,' said Fing.

In the control room was a man. He was slouched in his chair. He had a cloth draped on his shoulder. Under the cloth was something round and lumpy, a satchel maybe.

I went over and said:

'Captain Digsby?'

The man stirred, and jumped clumsily from his chair.

'What?' he said.

'How do you do?' I said. 'I'm Captain Belemus Duck, and this is the Albatross's robot, X 16.'

'Eh?' said Captain Digsby.

He had deep black rings around his eyes and his cheeks were sunken to parchment.

'I'm on a rescue mission,' I said. 'To find you, Captain Digsby.'

The man stared at us.

'Go away,' he said.

'What?' I said.

'Go away,' he said, and stepped closer. He didn't touch me. 'Hurry.'

'I'd like to,' I said. 'With you of course.'

'No,' he said. 'Leave me here. I'll be free soon.'

'Fing,' I said. 'Is he ill? Can you ask the computer?'

'Affirmative.'

There was a buzzing from inside Fing.

'Captain Digsby has no disease,' the robot said. 'Suffering from malnutrition. Nothing else detectable.'

'Ha!' said Captain Digsby. 'Detectable! That's the word. But nothing here really is.'

'Captain, have you run out of food?' I asked. 'Is your food section broken?'

'Food,' said the Captain. 'Would you have me feed it then?'

'Feed who?' I said. 'Feed what?'

'Go away,' he said, and rushed from the room.

We followed him down the steps from the spacecraft. He sped over the blue grass and knelt by the sea. He started to gulp handfuls of water. I walked up behind him.

'Is that tasty?,' I said.

'What?' he said.

'The water,' I said. 'Do you recommend it?'

I bent down to taste it.

'Don't touch it!' he said. 'No!'

I didn't. I stood up.

'Captain, we must be going now. I suppose your ship is out of action?'

'Eh?'

'Your ship?'

'Yes, yes,' he mumbled. 'Quite useless.'

'Well,' I said. 'We need to transfer your freezer unit up to our ship. We've lost our second one. Fing,' I said, 'Can you see to that?'

123

'Affirmative,' said Fing.

Fing went back into the Cormorant. A little later he brought the freezer unit down and jetted up to the Albatross with it.

'Captain,' I said. 'I must ask you to accompany me to the sick-bay of the Albatross. You need attention. We must restore the effects of your malnutrition before you're put into deep freeze.'

'Don't go with him,' said a voice.

I wasn't sure where it came from. At first I thought it was from Captain Digsby, but I had been looking at his face and his mouth hadn't moved.

'Don't go,' the voice repeated.

'No!' said Digsby in reply. 'No, I'll stay. I'll stay!'

'Who are you talking to?' I said.

'What?' said the Captain.

'Look, Captain Digsby, pull yourself together. Are you a ventriloquist? Are you slightly mad? Who are you speaking with?'

'Ha ha,' said the tones. 'Don't tell him, don't tell him.'

'No!' said the Captain. 'No, no, I won't!'

He touched the cloth on his shoulder for a second. He made panting noises through his nose.

'May I look at your shoulder, Captain?' I said. 'What is that bump under the cloth?'

I reached out my hand to pull it away.

'Stop him,' the voice commanded.

Digsby jumped away, but he was too late. I had a grip on the cloth, and when the Captain moved, the cloth pulled off.

'Too bright, too bright, too bright,' said the shrunken head on Digsby's shoulder.

'Don't hurt him!' said the Captain, creeping back to me. 'Please, give me his cloth back. Please.'

'What is it?' I said.

'Nothing,' said the Captain. 'Go away. Give me the cloth.'

124

'Light hurts, light hurts, light hurts,' said the wrinkled face. It poked up on a short neck from the Captain's overalls.

Fing returned to my side.

'Freezer installed,' he reported. 'We are ready to leave, Captain Duck.'

'Fing,' I said, 'give me an analysis of the thing on the Captain's shoulder.'

Fing's insides whirred.

'Parasite,' he said.

'Where does it come from?'

'It grows from the Captain. It shares his body systems. It is taking the Captain over.'

Captain Digsby was at the water's edge again, scooping up liquid into his throat.

'Yes, yes, drink,' the head was whispering to him.

Captain Digsby turned round. For a moment he seemed more like himself.

'Leave,' he said. 'I'll deal with this. I'm starving myself. That'll fix him. Go away.'

'Where did you get it?' I said.

'The water,' said Digsby. 'The water. Drinking the water. The sea's full of them. Parasites. They get inside you. The head bloomed last week. I can feel him inside me. I'll finish him. Go away.'

'Captain,' I said. 'You have power over it for a few seconds. Come back with us to the Albatross. I think we can free you of it.'

When the Captain heard that, he grabbed the cloth from my hand, and draped it over the head again.

'I'm ashamed of it,' he said.

We hurried to the Link Ship and lifted to the Albatross. The Captain was gibbering with the strain of keeping control. I led him to the sick-bay and sat him in the time reversal machine. I hooked him up. Just as I had him strapped in, his control broke, and he started to scream out:

125

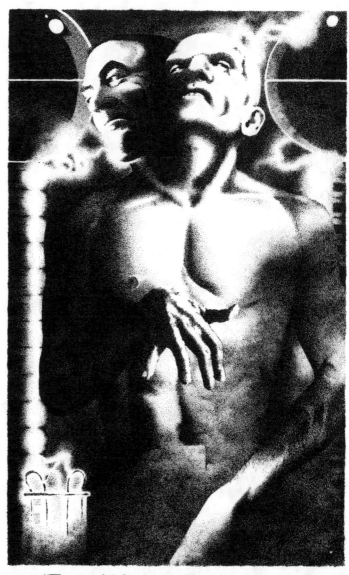

*"The captain's head grew big again, and the eyes of
the parasite closed"*

'No, no,' he said, 'don't hurt him, don't hurt him, don't hurt me!'

The cloth fell off. I saw the head swell, and Captain Digsby's features shrinking. The alien face was cased in blue skin. As the face swelled, the Captain's overalls began to rip, showing blue skin spreading down over his shoulder. I pressed the switches as quickly as I could. The Captain's head grew big again, and the eyes of the parasite closed. It shrank away to nothing. The health of the Captain restored, and the circles vanished from his eyes. A stream of water poured from his mouth onto the floor. A blue slug slithered in the pool of liquid.

'What's the computer say about this?' I said.

'No response,' said Fing. 'Alien matter. Not computable.'

'Start the incinerator,' I said.

I took up the squirming parasite with a long pincers, and threw the lot, pincers and all, into the flames. The dial registered annihilation.

The Captain's eyes opened. He was confused by his surroundings. He had many questions and we told him what we knew.

Fing brought him to the second freezer module – housed in the food room – and put the Captain in storage for the journey home.

I set the controls for Earth, and went with Fing to the sick-bay to be frozen too. It wasn't the sick-bay any more when I got there, it was the hall of my house.

Soon after that was my thirteenth birthday. I haven't had any adventures since – but I'm waiting.